Vatican File 1161. Galileo

I. T. Wyatt

I. T. Wyatt

Copyright © 2013 I. T. Wyatt

All rights reserved.

ISBN-10: 1515019071
ISBN-13: 978-1515019077

Vatican File 1181: Galileo

DEDICATION

To my dearest Sheila, without whose support, encouragement and love this book could not have been written.

I. T. Wyatt

Vatican File 1181: Galileo

CONTENTS

Acknowledgements...... vii

I

Rome 1616............... p.1

II

1624.................... p.70

III

1631.................... p.113

I. T. Wyatt

ACKNOWLEDGMENTS

I am grateful to the friends and relatives that have taken the time to read earlier drafts of *Galileo* and were kind enough to encourage me to continue. I am especially grateful to Father Gerard Hughes for his insights into faith and the Catholic world. I am also grateful to Murad Nazaraliev of Vito Technology for allowing me to use their image *Earth - Solar Walk*. Finally, but by no means least, a special thank you to my wife Sheila, without her constant encouragement and support I doubt I could have finished this book.

I. T. Wyatt

I

1
ROME 1616

Without another word, the cardinal strode across the room and pressed a letter into the man's hand; he moved with such authority that the three inquisitors did not dare to question him. The man understood his unbidden instruction to say nothing as Cardinal Bellarmino led him out of the library.

"Giuseppe," the cardinal called to his servant. "Take my guest back to his residence at the Villa Medici." As they approached the main door of the house, the cardinal ordered the man, "Keep this letter safe."

The cardinal paused politely at the open door as his guest passed by in silence without looking at his host, the letter imprisoned in his taut white fist. As Giuseppe pulled the door closed Cardinal Bellarmino returned to the library, his tense jaw altering the contours of his neatly trimmed beard. He determined to rid himself of these inquisitors as quickly as possible. He entered the library to an immediate stream of accusations from the leader of his unwelcome and uninvited guests.

"Your Eminence, I must protest. The Holy Office has given clear instruction that Signor Galilei is to be given this warning forbidding him from ever holding, discussing or propounding the view, contrary to Scripture, that the earth moves about the sun. Yet, you have allowed him to leave with only a letter of guidance." A gently raised hand silenced the chief inquisitor.

"You would do well to remember to whom you are speaking and that a letter from a cardinal carries all the legal force of Holy Mother Church. You should also be aware that I am acting on the instructions given to me personally by His Holiness. The failure of others to carry out tasks, as directed by their masters, is not my concern. I bid you Fathers goodnight." The calmly detached presence of the cardinal signalled that their discussion was at an end. The three Dominicans left, and with reluctant civility kissed the sapphire of the cardinal's ring of office.

The three members of the Congregation of the Holy Office, a usefully opaque title for the Inquisition, walked stiffly though the winter darkness of Rome under a cloudless sky. Father Giustino broke the silence. "Bellarmino is a fool and must surely pay for daring to impede us in our holy mission."

Turning sharply on his heel, the sound of his swirling habit cutting the night air, Father Baccarini admonished Giustino with a barely restrained roar. "Silence, you idiot." His face was so close that Giustino felt momentarily nauseated by the oppressive warmth and moisture of Father Baccarini's breath. In that instant, Father Pietro Giustino experienced the unalloyed fear of those he pursued. It was rare for Father Baccarini to become visibly angered: a man of angelic appearance with warm eyes, he usually wore a genuinely friendly visage that belied his passionate sense of duty. Indeed, it was said of him that he could draw a confession from a statue with only a look.

Father Baccarini turned away and resumed his march, announcing to the night and his companions, "His Eminence, Cardinal Bellarmino, is a man of great spiritual and intellectual integrity, a valued servant of Holy Mother

Church. You would be wise not to speak of him with such disrespect." After a few more strides, he added, "It could land you in a great deal of trouble."

The third man in the company, Father Marino, could not tell if it was the sharp February air or the ferocity of Baccarini's outburst that made him shudder. His only thought was to be back at the friary as quickly as possible; this evening had been a frightful mess and he felt scared. A half moon stood high in the western sky but offered little light for the travellers. The Black Friars walked along the Via del Corso and then followed the dark, relentless Tiber. They traversed the city, leaving a contaminating hint of suspicion in their wake that spread like ink in water. Neither Father Baccarini nor his companions were aware of Orion's bright sword suspended above them.

Father Baccarini strode a little ahead of his companions. He considered Giustino and Marino too ignorant and officious to realize the subtle danger of their situation. To inform His Holiness of their failure would be to invite risky opprobrium but to report Bellarmino's actions might be interpreted as appearing to question His Holiness himself. A Tuscan and a Jesuit, the cardinal was widely known and respected; the Holy Office could risk offending neither the Medici family nor the Collegio Romano.

It took them about forty minutes to walk up to Santa Sabina at the summit of the Aventine Hill. Father Marino fell behind the others, breathing heavily as he struggled up the steep Clivo dei Publicii that led to the basilica. As they entered the vestibule Father Baccarini bid Father Giustino goodnight; Giustino went up to the cloister and across to the dormitory but Father Baccarini turned right and entered the basilica. The great, carved door groaned into the darkness. Father Baccarini could not see its carvings or the mosaic of Father Mañoz de Zamora in the nave but he knew every inch of the basilica, and the people depicted in these images offered him comfort as he knelt before the Blessed

Sacrament. It was not unusual for Father Baccarini to spend long hours in prayer; he did not find it easy to undertake the Lord's work. After an hour or so, a course of action was revealed to him in the lines of a Psalm: "The Lord is near to all who call on him, to all who call on him in truth". He would simply tell the Commissary General what happened at the cardinal's palazzo and suffer the consequences. He got up to retire, his mind now calm but his knees and legs shot through with hot pain: a small price to pay in the service of the church.

After worship at Prime, Father Baccarini waited in the garden adjoining the basilica for his two compatriots. Although still dark, the morning glow had begun to chase the darkness out of the sky. Pinpricks of light were visible in the city below, and the sound of mill workers beginning their labour joined the dawn chorus. The clear night had given way to low dark cloud, which invaded everything with its searching damp cold. Father Baccarini looked down on the impregnably black Tiber, it looked to him to be a vein of misery.

An uneasily cheery "Good morning" shattered his reverie. It was Father Marino, with the discomfort of yesterday behind him, who appeared determined to salvage something from their failure of the previous evening. Ignoring the silence that greeted him, Father Marino continued. "I am sure that when we explain the situation to the General we will not be held responsible for the actions of His Eminence." Father Giustino remained prudently quiet.

The few seconds that passed before Baccarini turned and responded felt like hours to Father Marino; his optimism evaporated completely in those tense moments. Father Baccarini spoke with gentle authority but the gloomy cold sharpened it to a Damascene edge. "I have decided that, as chief inquisitor, the responsibility for last night's failure is mine and mine alone." The others did not attempt to object or intervene. "I will report to the Holy Office, ensuring that no blame may attach itself to your roles in this affair. God's will shall direct the good offices of Holy Mother Church."

Father Giustino thought briefly about insisting that they should go together, but his memory of last night chased the idea away. He knew that Father Marino would want in his heart to support Baccarini but he was also aware that Marino did not have sufficient courage to speak his mind and he would always take the line of least resistance and stay out of trouble. So neither man spoke, but their relief was clear to each other when Baccarini broke the awkward moment by setting off down the steps towards the Tiber.

Father Baccarini walked along the river, resigned to accepting the punishment for his failure. But he was puzzled: he could not understand why he had been asked to deliver an order that Cardinal Bellarmino had also been asked to issue. He knew, only too well, that the administration of the Holy Office was too punctilious for this to occur by error. He drew level with Tiber Island, where he turned away from the river, past what had once been the Theatre of Marcellus, its curve of classical columns now adorning the palace of the Peruzzi family. As he walked, he became acutely aware of how the present is necessarily built on the past and that progress of any sort inevitably alters or destroys what has gone before. As he navigated the maze of tiny streets and their litter of churches, it began to rain heavily, and he reached the imposing structure of Santa Maria sopra Minerva thoroughly soaked. He entered, not the church but the neighbouring offices of the Inquisition and the Dominican Order.

A notary greeted Father Baccarini cordially and disappeared into the General's office. After a few minutes Father Baccarini became aware of an unpleasant odour rising from his wet habit. This was not something that had ever concerned him before but for some reason it now seemed to attack his senses and undermine his confidence. He turned the events of the previous evening over in his mind, but still he could not understand how two orders came to be issued for one man. The notary eventually invited Father Baccarini into the room. Commissary General Michelangelo Seghizzi barely acknowledged Father Baccarini, he mutely indicated that he sit. Baccarini glanced back as he did so and saw the notary close the door and seat himself at a small desk. This was worrying; his meetings with the General were not usually recorded, and there could be no other reason for the notary to be present. The General's harsh features suited his militaristic title. He was a man with empty eyes.

"Where are Fathers Giustino and Marino?" the General barked without looking up.

"Yesterday did not go as expected, General. Therefore, if there are consequences to answer I accept sole responsibility."

"Very commendable, I'm sure." General Seghizzi neither liked nor trusted thoughtful men and, despite Father Baccarini's exemplary service, he had always been suspicious of Baccarini's intellect. "Well get on with it, what happened?"

Father Baccarini related the events of the previous evening. "His Eminence Cardinal Bellarmino gave me no opportunity to question the accused or present the injunction to him. Indeed, he was quite emphatic that he was acting under the direct orders of His Holiness. Thus it was a letter from his Eminence Cardinal Bellarmino that was served, not the order I was sent to issue."

"You are absolutely certain that Cardinal Bellarmino stated that he was acting under the direct instruction of His Holiness?" The General was looking directly at Baccarini, but his eyes gave no indication of whether or not he could actually see him.

"Yes."

"Do you have the injunction?"

"Yes, but it has not been signed. I expect it should be destroyed."

"Give it to me. I'll decide what to do with it."

Father Baccarini was conscious of the scraping of the notary's busy scribbling. "General, in my fifteen years' service, I have never been aware of an incident such as this, where two orders have been issued independently. Which rather begs the question of how this has come to pass, and what should be done with the unsigned order."

Seghizzi ignored Baccarini's concerns, and asked irritably: "You are a loyal member of the Congregation of the Holy Office, who believes in defending the faith? Your orders came from this office and were approved in the proper manner. I presume you do not want to question His Holiness personally? I can see only one course of action here." Father Baccarini now realized that he could not be at fault without the Commissary General also being implicated. That was some relief, but then came the General's shocking plan: "You will do absolutely nothing."

Father Baccarini's lips parted slightly but no sound came out, his eyes widened: would there be no re-checking of the order? No enquiry? No discussion? No questioning of clerks? Certain that his eyes would reveal his anger he did not dare to meet the general's gaze, he knew how difficult it was to counter an accusation of disloyalty. Father Baccarini had always been painfully scrupulous about his administrative practices. Justice, he believed, demanded clear and tested information; this could only be maintained through a rigorous administration, without which the quality of information could not be verified. Thus, the quality of justice would suffer. The General's plan of doing nothing undermined, in a moment, his faith in the Congregation's unswerving administration and his role in the defence of the faith. However, he also knew he was in no position to argue, he was certainly not going to suggest that Pope Paul be questioned and Cardinal Bellarmino could hardly be questioned further on the matter. As the wider implications of this apparent mistake were beginning to filter through his mind, the general spoke again.

"Father Baccarini, under the circumstances I feel compelled to remind you of your vow of secrecy. Now I suggest you go and remind Giustino and Marino likewise, I do not want to hear of this again."

Baccarini left in silence. The downpour had abated. Father Baccarini had never before thought to draw a distinction between his love of the Almighty and his faith in the Holy Office, working on behalf of the Lord. Now his belief in the integrity of the Holy Office had been shaken, fragments of previous cases began to fly through his mind in a cacophony of disassociated details. A signed document is an object of recognized authority, but if an unsigned document with no authority may be linked to an individual then no one is safe from the caprice of the state.

He knew the other two brothers would be pleased at this outcome, and would continue their work in their efficient bovine manner. He, however, was no longer sure; this spectre of doubt cast a long creeping shadow over his vocation. As he walked across a deserted Piazza Collegio Romano, it occurred to him that whilst the world might perceive the Vatican as the heart of Christendom, and Jerusalem its soul, he knew that the mind and conscience of Holy Mother Church actually rested in the two buildings he now stood between: Santa Maria sopra Minerva and the Collegio Romano. These seats of Dominican and Jesuit learning that guided, defended and promulgated the teachings and ordinances of the Church. The wealth and trappings of power, he thought, serve as much to deceive the viewer as to the actual location of power as they do to signal the personage of power.

2

As Father Baccarini waited to see the Commissary General, Cardinal Bellarmino was preparing to leave for an audience with His Holiness. The pouring rain added to his irritation of the previous evening, as he had hoped to enjoy a brisk walk up the hill to the Palazzo del Quirinale. Despite his seventy-four years, Roberto Bellarmino took every opportunity to rid himself of the accoutrements of office and he considered walking a reflection of the principled and simple life he aspired to live. So it was with some reluctance that he asked Giuseppe to prepare his carriage. Cardinal Bellarmino had learnt to accept the great wealth of the Church as a political necessity, and did not let his own desire to emulate the simpler lives of the Church Fathers pollute his mind with a disdain for that wealth.

The cardinal was led into the pope's private suite. Before he could remove his biretta and offer his greetings, a familiar voice exclaimed, "Roberto! How good to see you. Come, come, join me for lunch. Would you like lunch? There is plenty here and," he added with a smile, "nothing too fancy." Pope Paul V did not have to learn the pontifical habit of piling questions together, finishing other people's sentences and manipulating conversations.

"Your Holiness is too…"

"Now let's have none of that, we have known each other too long, and we are quite alone."

"As you wish, Camillo."

Despite their long friendship, Camillo Borghese paid Cardinal Bellarmino a great honour by greeting him in such an informal way, but it would be unwise for Bellarmino to forget the exalted position of his friend. They had known each other for almost twenty years and Camillo had been pontiff for half that time. With a round head, and seemingly no neck, Camillo presented more like a boxer than the apostolic Bishop of Rome. A daintily preened beard did little to counter the overall impact of his pugilistic features.

They ate bread, cold meats and fruit with a little wine next to a window that offered a panoramic view of the city. Today everything was grey; the rain beat a hypnotic rhythm on the window. "How did it go with our troublesome mathematician?" Camillo enquired with a full mouth.

"Not quite as planned." Bellarmino took another sip of wine, dabbed his mouth with a fine linen kerchief and prepared himself to detail the events of the previous evening. "Before I could deliver my order to Signor Galilei I found myself entertaining three Dominicans, who insisted that they also had an injunction to serve on him. Had our orders been identical I could have simply issued one and dismissed the other as an embarrassing mistake. Unfortunately, however, there was a slight but significant difference between the order we agreed, and the one presented by the Dominicans. In essence, where we had discussed the possibility of allowing Signor Galilei to make use of the Copernican theory as a mathematical hypothesis, the Inquisitors were demanding a complete prohibition on him ever making use of the hypothesis in any way whatsoever. Furthermore –"

"Which order was he given? I dare say you lost your temper and threw them all out, or did you sit and debate the finer points of all this nonsense? Which defender of the faith was sent to you?" Camillo asked, barely disguising his amusement.

"Father Baccarini." Bellarmino fought to keep his indignation at the pope's casual attitude out of his voice. "I gave my order to Galilei and then ushered him out before the Dominicans got their teeth into him; they were understandably annoyed at not being able to carry out their task. And I must confess to being more than a little perplexed by these events. There is no doubt that Baccarini's documents were in proper order, and I might add that I considered theirs the better of the two orders."

"But you did not let the Black brethren issue their injunction?"

"Your Holiness may recall that I was acting under your express instruction. Had your Holiness wished otherwise, I am sure it could have been arranged. I fail to see why we are treading so lightly with Galileo when the Congregation of the Index have suspended the books of Copernicus and Father Foscarini, works that he is clearly sympathetic to."

"Do I detect a hint of reproach in your voice? You think the warning you gave too soft?"

"No, your Holiness, please accept my humble apologies. It is the sin of pride you hear: I am proud of the labours of the Society of Jesus in restoring Holy Mother Church from the dark schism, and I am perhaps too hasty in my desire to defend those efforts and Holy Mother Church. It is my most sincere prayer that the Word of Scripture will never be abused."

The pope's response was measured and indulgent. "Of course, the Jesuits have provided Holy Mother Church with many saints in their defence of Scripture. But this situation, as I am sure you are aware, reaches far beyond the Collegio Romano into the visceral world of politics and patronage." He paused to give Bellarmino time to look suitably ashamed. "Phillip of Spain, Leopold of Austria and, of course, Duke Cosimo de' Medici are all supporters of Galileo, they are also close to the heart of the Bishop of Rome. Even here in Rome Galileo has his admirers, such as Prince Cesi and Cardinals Orsini and Barberini. A trial could embarrass some very powerful people, and Holy Mother Church is in no position to lose friends. Have you actually considered what a trial would entail?" Bellarmino was almost beside himself at such a condescending question. "Evidence would be brought to bear, and although Galileo has no evidence he would undoubtedly attempt to question the interpretation of Holy Writ in court."

"Men have felt the sharp tongue of fire for less," replied the cardinal with casual coldness.

"His Beatitude Clement VIII kept that friendless madman Bruno in chains for seven years before putting him to the stake. I have no intention of making a martyr of this mathematician, and offending half the world's most powerful and faithful nobles into the bargain. The Holy Office may be weak from our struggles with Luther's followers, but we maintain the role of sole interpreters of Scripture; this fine achievement of the Council of Trent we will not put at risk." The pontiff's voice was firm but strained.

Bellarmino could contain himself no longer. "So is the Word of Our Lord now to be subject to political expediency?"

Pope Paul appeared to pour his rage into his white fists and continued with creaking calmness. "Be thankful, Eminence, that I know you better than your words. No, at this stage we must try to silence Galilei by other means, and if we disabuse his theories in public his support will soon wane." He thought for a moment and continued speaking in a slow measured tone. "It was I that arranged for the three Dominicans to go to your home."

Bellarmino's restraint broke at this revelation and he cast aside any recognition of his inferior position. "What? Do you not trust me? Do our years of friendship mean nothing?

Am I now some clerk or ignorant officer to be tricked into your bidding?"

The pope's response was almost a whisper. "You were not informed of the other order because I wanted you to be angry when you saw them, I wanted that anger to be genuine so as to suggest to Galileo that you could be a useful ally to him."

"But what if the Dominicans had given their order?"

"I know you too well for that, my friend," replied Camillo.

"But why Baccarini? He will be suspicious and could cause trouble if he suspects that the Congregation has been used in some subterfuge."

"Unfortunately I left that choice to General Seghizzi, but if it proves to be a problem I am sure we can deal with it. I have no doubt that Signor Galilei will have been sufficiently worried by last night's events to never consider breaking the terms of his order. In which case, he is effectively silenced. However, if he should be foolish enough to continue propagating his theory he will probably contact you for advice. In any event we are now in a position to bring him to trial on the sole basis of the order, should he give us reason to do so."

"Will the sword of Damocles really keep him silent?"

Camillo's response was curt. "It usually does in my experience, he will surely be only too aware of the weak thread of hair which holds the sword from his fate. I dare say he is familiar with the Bruno affair and the mere thought of the stake will do our work for us. In addition, as a leading light of the Collegio Romano I am sure you will be able to arrange suitable lectures to present more orthodox views of the cosmos." This was offered as neither request nor order, it was a statement of fact.

Bellarmino recognized his cue and responded with due deference. "Of course, your Holiness. Did you wish to discuss anything further?"

"I have received a number of requests to grant this Tuscan an audience, what would you advise?" Bellarmino winced slightly at the way in which the pope managed to make "Tuscan" sound blasphemous.

"As you are trying to achieve the apparently contradictory ends of both threatening Signor Galilei and making him feel secure, I am sure that an audience with your Holiness could only help in securing the desired outcome." Although he despised this sort of political sophistry he was quite prepared to resort to it, if the mood took him. It was the Cardinal and not the friend that took his leave of the pontiff.

The downpour had faded to a light drizzle. Bellarmino sent Giuseppe away with instructions to collect him for Vespers from the Collegio. Even for a man of Bellarmino's advanced age it was a walk of only fifteen or twenty minutes down the hill and along the narrow Via dell' Umiltà. The small cobbled road had been transformed into a tiny river by the morning's rain, but the Cardinal lost none of his dignity and cared not for his sodden feet. He considered such minor sufferings to be good for his soul and integrity. It was no bad thing for the people of Rome to see men of his position getting their feet wet from time to time.

He climbed the few steps of the left portico in to the Collegio, passing under its directive motto of work *by religion and good skills*, and entered the scholars' courtyard. Today it was quite deserted but on bright sunny days it rang with the song of debate between students. The courtyard had been modelled as a cloister, which served as an architectural reminder of the dual function of the Collegio Romano as an institute of learning and defender of faith. In Cardinal Bellarmino's eyes it was the very nexus of spiritual and physical truth. He had a private study on the upper floor, near the secret library to which only select Fathers had access. The study was not large but it suited his tastes; he always felt comfortable and at ease there. He removed his biretta, hung his wet mantle on the door and put on an old habit. A desk sat under the window and benefited from the light and the view. It looked directly on to the palazzo of Cardinal Aldobrandini. Bellarmino quietly enjoyed musing on the contrasts and contradictions between the grandeur of the palazzo he sat opposite, private and public struggles for knowledge, and the ideal of holy orders.

Secure in the warm womb of his room, he looked through the insights of the Church Fathers, searching for some justification for embarking on a dissembling friendship. But he could see only incoherent collections of letters, and although he knew these books well, the words fell into his eyes and disappeared without meaning. After some hours, he stopped looking for specific books and sat vacantly picking up piles of words for his eyes to dance across. He picked up St. Augustine's *De Genesi ad Litteram* for the second or third time. As he leafed through the pages, his attention was caught by a warning on any philosophical teaching that may be contrary to the teachings of the Church and scripture. Faced with such writing, he read, a man should "without any doubt believe it to be completely false"; his eyes and mind were instantly attuned. His Holiness was quite wrong: *Genesis*, *Ecclesiastes* and *Joshua* all state that the sun moves around the earth and this should be enough to bring Galileo to trial. However, Pope Paul had made up his mind. Unlike many Cardinals, duplicity did not come easily to Bellarmino.

A sudden thud startled him. He turned to see his wet mantle fallen to the floor. He stared at the pool of crimson and it put him in mind of another despoiled robe, that which carried the blood of Christ. Bellarmino began to realise that he need not view his personal distaste at establishing a potentially mendacious relationship with Galileo as an intellectual question, but a matter of faith, theology and the greater good. He recalled the Bull issued by Pope Paul III at the founding of the Society of Jesus, that the Order "will fight for God and God alone under the banner of the cross". Humbled by his vision, he thought of Holy Mother Church and the insignificance of his own discomfort at forming a dishonest relationship. Yes, he thought, I will present a friendly face of support to Signor Galilei whilst ensuring that the Truth seeks him out and silences him.

3

After taking his leave of Cardinal Bellarmino, Galileo's carriage travelled north to Piazza del Popolo before the road twisted up the hillside and turned southwards to the Villa Medici; a long enough journey for the pleasing scent of the woods to fill his nose and for the cold night air and rough road to attack his arthritic joints. At least the pain kept his fear at bay. He could not believe that barely a week had passed since his fifty-second birthday. In that short time he had descended from welcome and energetic visitor to the nobility to a decrepit old man with joints full of sand. How different this was to his last visit to Rome.

His ears filled with the sound of approving chatter, laughter, applause and the adulation of Roman society; fine food, fine wine, beautiful women with pleasing smiles and more than the occasional warm caress. However, his moment of crowning glory came in the lecture theatre of the Collegio Romano. Professor Clavius spoke, in a hall crammed with the intellectual and clerical elite of Rome and the Vatican, and publicly supported Galileo's observations of the stars of Jupiter, the surface of the moon and the phases of Venus described in his new book *The Starry Messenger*. Galileo felt himself glow a little at his recollection of the public praise from the chief astronomer and mathematician of the Society of Jesus. But this soon disappeared as he also recalled how the evening was almost ruined by some idiot student. As the proceedings were drawing to a close, a young man called out from the back of the hall.

"Professor Clavius, your Eminences, please excuse this crass interruption but I must ask Signor Galilei a question of the utmost pertinence." Galileo shuffled on his seat, irritated that anyone should have the temerity to want to question him and attempt to spoil his evening.

"Please be silent and return to your seat. Questions are not permitted during orations," declaimed Professor Clavius as he attempted to conclude the matter of the evening.

The man persisted. "Then I must release my question for all your ears with no expectation of a response. How does Signor Galilei reconcile his views, and those of Copernicus, with those of Aristotle? Are they not mutually exclusive? Surely he is aware that to undermine Aristotle is to undermine the teachings of our Holy Mother Church, Scripture, this very Society of Jesus? This cannot be a Catholic position."

"Please keep the manners of the market in the market," Clavius demanded, "or if you cannot do so then remove yourself."

Galileo's anger and indignation, fuelled in part by wine, drove him to stand up and respond without invitation. "If I may be so bold, Professor? We cannot blame a pup for being able to see only its mother's teat, and perhaps when the pup is old enough to see past the pap it may be able observe more than it can grasp." The room exploded with laughter and the audience dispersed in high spirits. Galileo could see from Clavius' stiff and deliberate movement that he was furious; he assumed that this was because a student demeaned the Professor's role in assessing Galileo's work. He did not realise that in fact Professor Clavius was angry at his conferee,

Galileo, that he should insult the Society by responding to a student in such a foul and puerile manner.

The babble of laughter and chatter continued as the gathering left the oration and poured out into Piazza Collegio Romano. Galileo strolled down Via Pie' di' Marmo with Cardinal Maffeo Barberini. The sun had not quite set and the slither of a new moon presented itself in the west; high in the deepening cyanic sky the pinprick of Jupiter was presiding over Orion and his companions. Maffeo slipped his arm through that of Galileo's and held it firmly. "My dear friend, that was the most shameful example of bitter exhibitionism I have seen in some years."

Galileo, like a child, feigned ignorance. "What are you talking about?"

"His Eminence, Cardinal Bellarmino, does you the honour of convincing the Collegio Romano that they should certify your discoveries, and you repay his interest and generous support with a vicious attack on Signor delle Colombe and insult the Society of Jesus in the process. What on earth has delle Colombe done to you to deserve such an outburst?"

"Who?" asked Galileo mischievously.

"The young man that reasonably, if rudely, asked about Aristotle and whom you insulted. Do you mean to say that you have never before met him and yet you publicly humiliated him? And in the Collegio Romano of all places, do you intend to make an enemy of every mathematician in the Church?"

Galileo pulled his arm out, stopped and turned to face his friend. "That rich fool deserved every word and more. What idiotic rubbish he spoke and how dare he question my observations, interpretations and worst of all my faith! Quite intolerable!"

"Did he? Are you able to reconcile your views with those of Aristotle?" chided Maffeo. "But tell me, do you declaim him to be a fool for being rich or for holding a different view? Which is the more offensive?"

Galileo started walking again and replied sulkily, "Now who demeans himself? As you know only too well, wealth in the abstract is of no consequence. It is what one does with the opportunities it provides that is important. Men like your good self or Prince Cesi use your wealth and position to improve the minds and souls of others."

"And agree with you," Maffeo interjected.

"Well, yes, and why not? Fools like that man view their wealth as an opportunity to parade themselves as right by virtue of being rich, they contribute nothing new, they regurgitate the works of others without expending any effort in actually thinking about them, indeed they have a vested interest in maintaining the status quo. If Aristotle stood in front of that man and said: 'I have changed my mind about the four elements; there are actually five' or eight or none, he would say 'but that is not what you had previously written, you have obviously lost your reason'. His kind ask a question not to elicit a greater truth but to confirm their own position. His casual confidence belies an arrogance of immense proportions."

"I see, and your attack on him was the measured response of a modest and moderate man?"

Galileo, recognizing the truth of Maffeo's comments, spoke softly in reply. "It is true I probably did respond harshly, but it is the fire of conviction that drives me. Surely you understand that?"

"Yes, but where the approval of Professor Clavius is always measured and of great worth, that of Prince Cesi and the Linceans is at best a mixed blessing. So you should make every effort to maintain the support of the Society of Jesus."

"What do you mean? I thought the Linceans to be made up of intellects of the greatest integrity and insight; they invited me into the Academy and financed the publishing of my book. It is such a rare pleasure to meet and discuss the nature of the world with a group of men capable of intelligent conversation that is based on learning and observation rather then mere recitation. Indeed the prince,

Federico, actually said that we should be 'slaves neither of Aristotle nor any other philosopher, but of noble and free intellect in regard to physical things'." His pride broke into laughter. "Oh, and such good humour they share; only last week, at a celebratory dinner in my honour, mark you, they coined a new name for my spyglass: the telescope. I think they thought a Greek compound name for my instrument amusing given that it will be the demise of the ideas of that greatest of ancient philosophers. No, you must be mistaken about any concerns from that quarter, I can assure you."

Maffeo responded in sombre tones, his face as cold and unmoving as marble. "No, Leo, I am afraid that you do not understand the situation at all. You are flattered by these men, you are amused in their courtly company, but you do not know them and you do not know Rome. Your voice has been given just promotion but you cannot have heard the serious rumours that abound about these men."

"Ah, rumours, the stories of fishwives and drunkards, such empty words are of no interest to me," Galileo said loudly.

"Don't be naïve, Leo. An interesting little rumour has much longer legs than the dull truth and is capable of far more damage. The rumours attached to these men are particularly salacious and are unlikely to go away, no matter how little truth they may contain. It has been said that their interests are actually those of the occult black arts, that they live hedonistic lives of fornication and that they are utterly opposed to the doctrines of Holy Mother Church."

"Maffeo, I am surprised at you listening to such silly nonsense. Prince Cesi is a man of the most erudite intellect and propriety and I am proud to be considered a friend of his."

"Leo, you listen, to me, now," snapped Cardinal Barberini. "I am as certain as you that these stories are nonsense, but truth is not the issue here. I have no doubt that if charges were brought against any of these men they would quickly and easily be proved innocent on just about any matter except that of opposition to Church doctrine. This is a rumour that has the ability to stick to one under any circumstances and how does one prove that one is not opposed to a doctrine? This, my friend, is the most pernicious and dangerous of the rumours surrounding your new friends; this alone is reason enough to keep a friendly but polite and respectable distance from them. We both understand that conviction can drive a man to the fire of the stake." Maffeo placed his hand firmly on Galileo's shoulder. "Leo, you must learn to temper your responses . Professor Clavius may have spoken well of your work but delle Colombe's question was not unreasonable. Furthermore his position represented the views of many men in the Collegio Romano; when speaking from within the very bosom of the Jesuit world it is only wise to treat their views with due decorum. An episode like this evening's could cost you dearly, my friend. Learn to temper your temper or it will try you."

Galileo's reverie was broken by the sharp turn of the carriage in the courtyard of Villa Medici. Giuseppe helped him out of the carriage and up the half-dozen or so marble steps of the villa. A high arch with flanking pillars announced to the world that this was the home of a powerful family and that the visitor should be proud, or daunted, to be associated with such wealth and power. Galileo thanked Giuseppe and invited him to have some warm broth before returning home. A small portal within a large door opened in the vast vault and Galileo was greeted with a look of concern from the master of the house, Francesco Niccolini, the Florentine ambassador to Rome.

"Leo! My goodness, you look ill, are you unwell? Come in, sit, let me get you something."

"Please do not trouble yourself," replied Galileo shakily. "I am just a little weary. Perhaps Giuseppe could go down to the kitchen and warm himself?"

"Of course." Francesco had Giuseppe led away and ordered wine for his guest.

Galileo sat on a couch in the warm sanctuary of a huge fire. "Actually, perhaps I could have a little wine?"

Francesco's wife, Caterina, joined the two men by the fire, a graceful beauty with pale skin and bright eyes, a most suitable match for the ambassador. As Galileo thawed, he felt the pain of his arthritis begin to ebb and his cheeks start to flush: the pallid grey of death left his face.

"So, how was your visit with his Eminence the Cardinal?" Francesco asked, after a polite pause and the arrival of the wine. Galileo focused his attention on the fire and addressed the flames.

"The evening started well. However, once the pleasantries were over, his Eminence informed me that the Congregation of the Index have suspended Copernicus's book, and that Father Foscarini's book has been banned. I had, of course, heard rumours that any discussion of the earth's motion about the sun was likely to have a difficult reception, but to be banned by the Index is dangerously close to being considered heretical. I was so shocked by this news I didn't know how to reply. There is no hiding the implicit support of the Copernican hypothesis in *The Starry Messenger*, but am I now to be considered a heretic? I don't mind admitting to you, my tongue was frozen with fear and rage at those accursed so-called philosophers of the Collegio Romano. That bastion of knowledge functions only to smother modern thought with Aristotle's gown." His gaze left the fire as he sat back in the couch and raised his glass to his hosts, he saw but did not recognize their shock at his outburst; such bile was unusual even for him. Now addressing Francesco and Caterina, he continued. "I tried to explain to his Eminence that it has never been my intention to embarrass the church, on the contrary, I want to prevent any possible future embarrassment. Bellarmino simply droned on about the *Book of Joshua*, and informed me that the advisors to the Index found that it demonstrated that the earth is stationary and it is the sun that moves, as indeed can be seen every day. Scripture, he said, precludes any consideration of theory. He spoke as though I had never read *Joshua* and that any theological arguments I may offer are worthless. That such men should blindly adopt a literal reading of Scripture is folly verging on madness. The fact that the sun appears to move across the sky, in the eyes of every peasant and lord, is not an argument against astronomical observation and mathematics." Galileo's speech tailed off into a private reverie of anger.

"Leo, you are our finest philosopher, I am sure you will soon have an appreciative audience," interjected Caterina soothingly. She walked over and sat next to him, like a mother with an upset child.

"Alas, my dear Caterina, I think not. I informed his eminence that I have never considered myself a theologian and would always bow to the church on theological matters, but that this is not a theological matter. I tried to explain to him that the purpose of my work is," he spoke more calmly now, at a distance from himself, "to understand the work of the omnipotent Craftsman." He sipped some wine, then disappeared into the flames again. "Bellarmino told me he had asked to see me at the personal instruction of His Holiness. To give me a written order not to hold or espouse the Copernican theory, but that I may refer to it as a hypothesis, a false one, mark you, when considering astronomical calculations. Before I could respond to this order, we were joined by three Dominicans from the Inquisition."

Francesco and Caterina sat wide-eyed at this news. The only sound and movement in the room was that of the ever hungry fire. "It seems that the Black brethren were also instructed to issue an injunction to me, but theirs was to say that I could not discuss or even consider the motion of the earth as a hypothesis. I was to be silenced completely. An undignified dispute then waged between these pillars of Holy Mother Church as to which order I was to be subjected to; they were like dogs fighting over a bone. However, fortune and the Cardinal were on my side as he had already prepared his order. He unceremoniously thrust the missive at me and marched me out of the house. The church and her scurrying lawyers are so proud of the Congregation of the Inquisition, and yet they cannot agree on how to proscribe me."

"Do you have the letter?" asked Francesco. Galileo reached into his doublet and carelessly passed him the ball of paper which Francesco then carefully unfolded and smoothed on his thigh. "It is interesting to see that you are ordered to 'abstain from propounding' and 'not to defend', but there is no mention of heresy. This is an oddly short letter for such an important debate. It seems to me, you should be quite safe with this document to vouchsafe your lectures," pronounced Francesco authoritatively.

"I am afraid you miss the point, my friend; there is no debate in their eyes. But it is strange that you should use the word 'safe'. As I was leaving the Cardinal's house he told me that I should take care not to lose this letter." He returned his gaze, his eyes vacant and hopeless, to the spitting, snapping fire which also concealed the slightly desperate sound of fear in his voice.

"My husband reads with the dry calculus of a lawyer, I am sorry to say." Now Caterina spoke with authority. "Leo, you cannot dismiss this evening as an administrative blunder; it is extremely rare for the Inquisition to err in their processes. Also, and please forgive me, Leo, you have been a cause of some embarrassment to Jesuit intellectuals for years; there seems to be no doubt that they want you silenced. You have been given a clear warning here and not to heed it would be tantamount to suicide."

"Caterina! How can you speak to our distinguished guest so?"

"Dear husband, please hear me out. The Index has suspended the very writers from whom Leo draws support, and you can be sure that they will most assuredly be considered heretical writers. Leo is a threat to the ecclesiastical intelligentsia. If this warning is ignored or contravened in spirit, let alone in word, it will bring disaster down on our honoured guest and friend."

Galileo sat transfixed by Caterina's lips; the moist motion of her tongue on her teeth as she spoke, certain that each utterance was borne on the breath of sincerity and truthfulness. He suddenly ached for the company of a woman; he missed the reassuring embrace of another's arms. He felt quite alone, and desired to be alone. "Francesco my friend, I am afraid that we find ourselves having to be humbled by the wisdom of womanhood. Caterina is, I am sure, quite right. Indeed some might say I have only myself to blame, that I have squandered my previous good relations with eminent and influential Jesuits such as Professor Clavius. But they will persist in conflating theology and natural philosophy when this should not be within the magisterium of the church."

Federico did not respond to this admission of Galileo's. "Are you still hoping for an audience with the Pope?"

"If I am granted an audience I can hardly turn it down, but there is no hope His Holiness will intervene in tonight's developments as they were his orders." Galileo wanted to get away from this discussion as it seemed to be heading down a road he felt he could not face: the abandonment of his advocacy of a heliocentric universe. Galileo slowly rose to his feet and with minimal courtesy left his friends by the fireside.

During his stay at the Villa Medici Galileo was given a room near the top of the north tower. This was not a room that the Niccolinis would normally consider suitable for an honoured guest, but it had easy access to the upper terrace, which served as an observatory for Galileo. The Niccolinis always ensured that a fire was kept in, and arranged for seats and a brazier to be put on the terrace for Galileo's comfort. Every step of the stairs required a monumental effort; he felt profoundly tired and did not even undress before getting into bed. However, once in bed he found he could not sleep, his mind wandering between the night's events, Caterina's warning, her fine features, the mother of his children, the price of truth. Could Venus have tricked him the way she did every idiot blinded by lust? Did he really see the planet's phases, like those of the moon, or could it have been an optical illusion? A mistake? It would be almost Prime, the coldest part of the night, when Venus appeared over the horizon and he would have less than two hours to make his observations before the sun and the he-goat pursued her out of the sky.

He decided to check the weather to see if it was at least worth staying awake. He climbed the tight spiral staircase and stepped out onto the balcony, a damp westerly stabbed at his joints and he cursed the breeze. "Elijah's right, the Lord is not in the wind." He looked towards Mount Cavo in the south-east but the wind was bringing a gift of clouds. He watched the clouds and intermittent stars for a while before retreating back to bed.

Unable to sleep, he re-read the last letter from his beloved Virginia. Her love and youthful vigour poured off the page, filling his eyes with water. It was now only a matter of months before she would take her vows at the convent. He was in no doubt about the strength of her faith and desire to serve God. She had written to tell him that when she took her vows she would adopt the name Suor Maria Celeste. He was proud of his daughter, but grieved at the loss of his favourite child to the same church which now troubled him so. For the first time in years, he missed her mother, Marina, and her generous flesh. He longed for the freedom of Padua and the lively debate that was encouraged in Venice. That was another lifetime, enjoyable, good, free, but, he reminded himself, it was a poor and Aristotelian life. He had chosen to observe nature before attempting to describe her, but many of his fellow philosophers did not want to look with their own eyes, they preferred to trust the vision of ancients to perceive the world.

Galileo awoke late to the sound of rain attacking the windows. Despite the downpour, he went up on to the terrace. He looked down on the Roman wall that ran near the villa, his eyes following its line to where it turned sharply north-west and appeared to move away from him into the distance. He knew, of course, that the wall encircled Rome and that a more modern spur branched off on the other side of the Tiber to enclose the Vatican. What an irony it is, he thought, that the hearts of both pagans and Christians should have been enclosed in the same compound. There were few people going about their business in the deluge. It was clear to him, as Caterina said last night, that any further conflict with Holy Mother Church, no matter how well intentioned, could end in death. Although a man of faith and integrity, he could not see that a theory, which he was certain was correct, was worth the sacrifice of his own life. His friends and patrons would not be able to save him from the Inquisition if they pursued their case more forcefully. He turned his face towards the leaden sky and let the rain wash down him. If this is where the River Acheron lies, he thought, I will not give these imbeciles the pleasure of paying the ferryman for me.

4

Winter tumbled into spring; Galileo eschewed the company of wealth and power. On the days that he felt inclined to leave the villa he would travel south of the city, through the Porta San Paolo, to spend his time in conversation with artisans and engineers. He loved the smell of industry and the language of manufacture. He found the observational knowledge, practical experience and honest language of metalworkers, engineers and glass-makers infinitely more useful and interesting than the bookish learning of his court peers. The insights of these men were based on experience and observation that Galileo respected despite their so-called uneducated status; he found their conversation stimulating and original in a manner that he thought most court philosophers would neither accept nor understand. But even here Galileo was a prisoner of his own tongue; he could not afford to enter into public philosophical debates. Such discussions inevitably arrived at the question of the position of the sun or the motion of the earth and he would struggle to remain silent. He was hiding in a different crowd. But it was not simple fear of the Inquisition that kept Galileo away from public debate. He no longer had the stomach for debates about astronomy and could see no future for his work. He had been effectively condemned to re-work older ideas and forced to shackle his imagination and perspicacity.

As the weeks passed Galileo became increasingly withdrawn and restricted himself to the Villa Medici. He confided to Francesco one bleakly despondent day that, "I may as well rip out my own eyes, before my patron disowns me."

Galileo arranged, without consulting his host, for a servant to visit his room at noon each day to receive instruction. Sleep was his only goal and when it evaded him Galileo wandered around the roof terrace; he would spend hours staring at moss clinging to the side of a brick, or along the line of coping on the balustrade, his eyes wandering between the pattern of the balusters and the distance, or at clouds passing over the countryside: on anything that focused his attention but did not engage his mind. His days were lost in vacant stares.

Francesco had been avoiding the delicate subject of their guest's unusual behaviour but Caterina's concern for Galileo would not allow him to remain a passive host. "Francesco, it has now been more than a week since we last saw Leo. Do you not think we should do something?" demanded Caterina.

"I went up to see him yesterday, he is unwell. You know he has great trouble with his joints and suffers regular bouts of fevers. I thought of sending for a physician but he told me not to, reminding me that he knew as much as any physician, and that all he needed was rest, warmth and hot food. Though, he did brighten up when I gave him the letter from Virginia."

"Oh, how he loves that girl. Did you tell him about the rumours?"

Francesco squirmed at this enquiry and left the table; he prodded the fire with a concentration it did not deserve. "Well?" she pressed.

"How could I? Our honoured guest is ill in bed. Do you expect me to worsen his condition by keeping him informed of market gossip?" Francesco tried to conceal his anxiety under a veil of anger, but failed.

"But you must say something to him. Better for him to be told by a friend than read about himself in that scandal sheet the *Avvisi*. That would be unforgivable." Caterina crossed the room, and gently wrapped her arms about his waist, placing her cheek next to his from behind. Caterina, deeply concerned for Galileo and his children, spoke in a soft whisper: "We both know how dangerous unchecked rumours can be. If we do nothing, this seeping poison will surely do great injury to Leo. I am sure you and he could find a way to halt this infection, these lies that claim he has been questioned by the Inquisition. Surely, there must be something you can do?"

"I wish I could, but it would be unwise of me to meddle directly in this affair without the express permission of Duke Cosimo. I will speak to Leo as soon as he seems fit enough." Staring into the fire, each lost in their thoughts, they stood only a breath apart but occupied quite separate worlds. Francesco worried over the political ramifications of the rumours and the fact that Galileo was under his roof. However, he could not wish his friend and countryman away. Besides, Caterina would never forgive him if he did. Francesco broke the moment. "I will send messages to Cardinal Orsini and Cardinal Barberini requesting they join us for supper. They are both friends of Leo and between the four of us we are sure to find some solution. Even if Leo is not able to join us we can at least begin to plan how to counter these rumours."

"What rumours are these?" came a sudden enquiry from the far corner of the room. The comfortably merged couple snapped back to reality and stepped apart in momentary embarrassment, they had not heard Galileo enter.

"Leo, it's so good to see you up, you are obviously feeling a little better. Some wine? Broth? Please join us by the fire. How is Virginia?" Francesco slipped quickly into the diplomatic speech of an accomplished host, hoping to distract Galileo.

"Dear Francesco, you really know how to pack a hundred questions into a single breath. Yes please, I would love to join you in a glass of wine, and Virginia is fine thank you. Now, what about these rumours?" Galileo settled himself comfortably on the couch.

Francesco saw it as his role to oil the wheels of social intercourse, but when cornered he would not shrink from the responsibility of delivering bad news.

"Caterina, would you see to the wine and some food, please? Leo, I shall come straight to the point. Since your meeting with His Eminence Cardinal Bellarmino, word has travelled around Rome, in the daily news-sheet, that you have been censured by the Inquisition and forced to abjure. Now, before you explode with rage, I have given this a lot of thought and have come up with a plan for dealing with these lies." Much to Francesco's surprise, and relief, Galileo just sat quietly, his eyes dull and flat, his voice a resigned monotone.

"This news does not surprise me, I know there are many that envy my skill and vision, and perhaps even some who fear my intellect. I have no doubt that the source of this fairytale lives within the Collegio Romano, or some other Jesuit seat of learning."

Francesco interjected optimistically. "I thought we might invite Cardinals Orsini and Barberini for a meal, so the three of you could formulate a response to these rumours."

"Yes, we could do that. Ah, Caterina, thank you, this wine smells wonderful. You know, I have given my favourite daughter to the service of the Church; not some rusty old maid, but a vibrant girl whose devotion is sublime. Her faith gives me strength and strengthens my faith, which in the current circumstances requires a strong buttress. I cannot believe I am so near to being openly accused of heresy."

Silence now descended on them, during this awkwardness Francesco began to offer a soothing remark but Caterina stopped him with a glance.

"The difficulty with your plan," Galileo continued, "is that it may expose our friendly cardinals to risk, and they are good men with whom the future of the Church lies. No, we can't do that. I will visit Cardinal Bellarmino and ask for a written certification that clearly refutes the rumours. If he obliges, it will demonstrate to all that the rumours are not true and that I can count on his support. If not, then he will show his hand, and the water is even deeper than I feared."

"Leo, I am afraid that your plan is flawed in that it rests entirely on the assumption that a single letter will provide the substantive support you need against these rumours. That is not an assumption you can afford, in my opinion, to make." Francesco tried to gently provide Galileo with the benefit of his experience. A dear fellow who knew his friend's weaknesses, he was acutely aware that Galileo was no politician and that he could barely play the court game. But Galileo had made up his mind and the matter was closed.

The following day brought a clear sky with the brightness of sharp steel; it carried little warmth for body or soul. Galileo walked, slowly and uncertainly, to Cardinal Bellarmino's palazzo. Like a disembodied soul, he watched his own progress from some undefined spot on high. He was thousands of miles away from the voices, rattles, snorts and shuffling feet of the busy streets. As he approached Cardinal Bellarmino's palazzo, to his surprise he saw the cardinal waiting at the door to greet him, biretta in hand. This answered any doubts he might have had about His Eminence; to be treated to such a public display of respect paid Galileo a great honour, which did not go unnoticed by those that could see.

"Signor Galilei, how lovely to see you. Please come in."

"Your Eminence is too kind," said Galileo as he kissed the cardinal's sapphire.

"Let us go through to the study. It is rather cosier than the library."

They entered a cell-like room, littered with books and papers; an oak chair displayed the roundels of the Medici crest. He had forgotten, if indeed he ever knew, that Cardinal Bellarmino was a fellow Tuscan. Galileo came straight to the point. "Your eminence, I have become aware that since our last meeting certain rumours have been circulating Rome to the effect that I have been reprimanded by the Inquisition and forced to abjure. I do not recognize this description of our meeting which, as I recall, centred on some recent decisions of the Congregation of the Index, and how I should take these into account in my work."

"Quite so," replied Bellarmino with a gentle nod.

"As you can imagine, I find these rumours to be hurtful, distasteful and injurious to my reputation. I have therefore come to humbly request that you write a statement to clear my name of these rumours and clarify our discussion."

Bellarmino did not reply immediately. He paused long enough for the silence to eat into Galileo, just enough to make him feel uncomfortable and remind him of the ever-present nearness of the Inquisition.

Eventually he spoke. "Of course, Signor Galilei, I quite understand the difficulty of your position and will write you a letter of certification immediately." He turned to his desk and began writing; at this Galileo felt his face relax involuntarily with almost overwhelming relief but he hoped, vainly, to avoid the embarrassment of Bellarmino seeing this. Cardinal Bellarmino continued speaking, whilst writing. "I know you are mindful of the Index, and I am sure that you would never knowingly claim anything in the Bible to be untrue."

"Of course not, Your Eminence," replied Galileo. But his hubris got the better of him, "We both know that the Bible is a guide for the spirit, and that its descriptions of the physical world are sometimes simplified so that those of a rude intelligence may be led to understand the greatness of

God. And that certain abstruse passages require intelligent and thoughtful consideration."

Bellarmino stopped writing and looked Galileo straight in his eyes. It was a piercing stare that touched Galileo's soul. The gaze paralysed him; his skin tingled as if every pore had a pin in it. He had gone too far. Cardinal Bellarmino spoke with forceful deliberation. "Signor Galilei, you may be a brilliant mathematician, you may even be the prize of Duke Cosimo's court, but you are not a theologian. I suggest you confine your brilliance to matters of the physical world and leave theology to those whose lives and hearts have been invested in the glory of the Church. Holy Mother Church expends great energies in fostering theological minds, and does not take lightly to those that would seek to undermine her efforts." Bellarmino returned to the letter.

Galileo wanted to reply with a tart comment about the risk theologians take by ignoring the observable world; that they could make Scripture appear false when they pass judgement on astronomical matters that they are not sufficiently skilled in observing and interpreting. He managed to control his urge to respond. Bellarmino's message was clear and unequivocal.

"There, I trust this will help put an end to those vile rumours." Bellarmino's tone was again friendly as he passed the letter to Galileo. "But where are my manners? May I offer you some wine, a little to eat?"

Galileo quickly opted for obsequious deference, which would allow him to reply to Bellarmino's warning, without making direct reference to it, and cast his eye over the letter.

"Your Eminence is too kind to a spiritual beggar such as I, and I have already taken too much of your valuable time." His eye fell on the passage he wanted to see: '...we say that the above-mentioned Galileo has not abjured in our hands, or in the hands of others here in Rome, or anywhere else that we know, any opinion or doctrine of his; nor has he received any penances, salutary or otherwise.' These words were enough to put a little light back into his eyes, and relief in his heart.

"Nonsense. However, I do have a number of other appointments this afternoon." Bellarmino scanned his desk, his fingers searching pieces of paper, apparently reminding himself of his other appointments; he was due to meet with Father Caccini later that day.

Galileo stood and made ready to leave. "Your Eminence has been most gracious in entertaining the worries of a poor scholar. But I should now leave, as I am sure Your Eminence has many more pressing matters with which to deal."

Bellarmino rose and extended his hand. Galileo bowed his head to kiss the cardinal's ring of office but Bellarmino held onto his hand a fraction longer than etiquette demanded. "We would like to offer you all the support we may. If you are in any doubt about possible theological matters that may arise in your work in future, you may contact us for advice."

"Thank you, I will most assuredly do as you have kindly offered."

As they walked along the corridor, Bellarmino told Galileo that Professor Grienberger was to give a lecture at the Collegio Romano next week, which he may find interesting. Galileo made a thoughtful-sounding response, but hoped beyond hope that the cardinal did not give him a direct invitation. He had been on good terms with Grienberger, they had even corresponded, but they clashed over the movement of the sun. He was sure the Jesuit professor would be offering a tired re-working of Ptolemy's description of the sun's movement with some brilliant but useless calculus on the apparently retrograde motions of the planets. Galileo could not risk being drawn into a public debate with an intellectual inferior and place his certificate from the cardinal at risk. To his great relief no direct invitation was offered.

Galileo decided that His Eminence Cardinal Bellarmino was a man he could trust and rely upon for support. He began to see a flicker of hope that he might be able to return to the motion of the earth and thus the cause of the tides in the not too distant future. Nevertheless, he wanted to leave Rome as soon as possible, and resolved to write to Duke Cosimo that very evening for permission to return to Florence.

***

A little after Galileo had left, Cardinal Bellarmino ordered his carriage to take him to see Father Caccini. He also decided to see His Holiness, as he was concerned that Galileo had not fully appreciated his warning. He arrived at Santa Maria sopra Minerva and spent a few minutes in prayer before speaking with the Master of the Convent. Father Caccini was a wily man with hungry eyes, and the cardinal disliked his naked ambition. Father Caccini greeted Cardinal Bellarmino with fulsome obsequity. "Your Eminence, I am honoured that you have seen fit to pray in our humble church."

The cardinal considered sopra Minerva anything but humble. In fact, he thought both the church and Master to be rather vulgar. "Father Caccini, I have come to see you on a matter of some delicacy that is of great importance to Holy Mother Church."

Caccini nodded gravely, but failed to conceal from the cardinal his euphoria at being given another chance to be close to Vatican politics.

"I will, of course, do whatever is within my meagre ability in the service of our Holy Mother."

"Yes, quite." Bellarmino could not resist agreeing with Caccini's mock modesty. "As it was you that initially brought Signor Galilei to the attention of the Congregation of the Inquisition and have spoken in sermons against him, it was thought that you could assist us further with this situation."

"In what way, Your Eminence?" Caccini could not keep his excitement and pride out of his voice, but he attempted to remain outwardly calm and concerned for the Church. This was his opportunity for further advancement, and that meant accepting the risks associated with becoming embroiled with the Inquisition and the machinations of the Vatican.

"We are mindful that it was through your good offices that certain questions with regard to Signor Galilei were brought to the attention of the Congregation of the Inquisition, but I must point out that any rumours you may have recently heard about Signor Galilei being questioned by the Congregation are, of course, false. Is that absolutely clear?" Father Caccini nodded sagely. The cardinal continued, "We can only hope that all of our shepherds are as astute as you, and your alacrity in this case has been noted. However, the situation is extremely delicate and His Holiness has charged me with the responsibility of ensuring that no future misunderstandings occur." Bellarmino paused but Father Caccini did not use the opportunity to ask for any clarification. "And so here I am today to ask you to continue to be mindful of the dangers of new knowledge. We would like you to give two or three sermons reminding your flock of the place of the sun in Scripture; you may also care to highlight the deficiencies of other suggested systems. However, you must not, under any circumstances, direct your comments to Signor Galilei personally. I cannot emphasize the delicacy of this situation strongly enough. Is this course of action acceptable to you?"

"Yes, of course, Your Eminence."

"Good. Signor Galilei is expected to be leaving Rome in the not too distant future, you simply have to dampen interest in discussions of any new and suspect theories. I do not need to remind you of the power of the pulpit of sopra Minerva; some may consider what you say to have come directly from the Congregation of the Inquisition, thus you must be very careful in your delivery. We would not want Signor Gallilei to suffer any further harm or indignation from misunderstandings that might flow from the pulpit."

"I understand. You can rely on me entirely, Your Eminence."

"Yes, of course," replied Cardinal Bellarmino coldly as he took his leave of Father Caccini. He had asked Giuseppe to wait for him, because although the day was bright he did not have the energy for the walk up the hill to Palazzo del Quirnale. The events of the past months had taken their toll on him, so he took the slower route through the crowded streets by carriage. Cardinal Bellarmino was not expected at the palazzo but was immediately admitted upon arrival, and ushered down the marble corridor to the pope's study. The silent purity of the building was defiled by the crashing boots of the Swiss guard and the cardinal striding along the enclosed walkway running between a vast luxurious garden and a stony courtyard. Cardinal Bellarmino explained to the pontiff's assistant that he had to see His Holiness as matter of urgency, and assured him that he would not take up much of the pope's valuable time.

"Roberto my dear fellow, what is this urgent matter?" Camillo's informal greeting gave Bellarmino his cue to dispense with formalities. Bellarmino waited until the assistant had left and closed the door before answering. "Signor Galilei came to see me this morning. He was concerned about the rumours that have been circulating about him having been admonished by the Inquisition."

"I see, and what was his disposition?"

"I think indignant is the term that best captures his mood. As we had discussed that I should encourage contact with him, I felt it necessary to be sympathetic towards him. After all, the rumours are untrue, irrespective of their source." Bellarmino risked this little flourish in the hope of discovering whether or not the Holy See was in fact the well from which the rumours sprang. The cardinal was to be disappointed; Pope Paul did not rise to the barb in his comment. "As Signor Galilei had not, technically, been admonished by the Congregation of the Inquisition, I thought the best course of action would be to enter his confidence by issuing a certificate denying the rumours. He was, of course, very pleased with this and I am confident he will correspond with me before printing anything contentious in future."

"Your course of action was absolutely correct, Roberto."

Bellarmino continued: "Unfortunately, I feel this may have compromised our position, in that he may no longer appreciate the full weight of the earlier warning. I thought that I should inform you immediately and, if Your Holiness permits, I would advise that you grant him a further audience to, how shall I say? Clarify the situation?"

"I see. Well, I can see him within the next couple of weeks, but you could have sent me a message about this. Is this really so urgent? Your face is full of worries."

"Holiness, I believe Galilei to be an extremely dangerous man and I fear that we have not been forceful enough in diverting him from his notions about a sun that does not move. He constantly undermines the work of Aristotle and so by extension much of the teaching of Holy Mother Church. We have managed to maintain the primacy of Holy Mother Church as the sole interpreter of Scripture largely through our educational establishments. If the curriculum we teach is under constant attack it will be seen by some as weakness and may lead to questions about, and challenges to, the authority of the exegesis of Holy Mother Church. Is this a risk we are willing to take?" Bellarmino allowed a few moments' silence for the pontiff to absorb his nightmare vision. He continued, "Signor Gallilei is obsessed with himself and his own vision, but I think if you were to grant him an audience your word would give us back the ground I relinquished this morning in keeping him silent."

In his best pontifical tone Pope Paul declared, "Our Lord is far greater than it is possible to imagine. Therefore, whatever men may say or claim to demonstrate is of no consequence: the Almighty is capable of acts that are beyond comprehension." Returning to Cardinal Bellarmino, he added, "Nevertheless, you are right to want Galilei directed towards some other philosophical vapour. Have you spoken to anyone else about this?"

"Not in any detail. I have instructed Father Caccini to continue his sermons but without directing his comments towards Galileo directly," replied Bellarmino.

"Good. I will deal with Galileo, and you should return to the contemplation of scripture."

"Of course, Your Holiness." The cardinal left with a great sense of relief, confident that the Pope would succeed where he may have failed. Furthermore, Roberto was now quite satisfied that an audience would direct any future questions about Galileo back to His Holiness and not himself.

5

Galileo received notification from the Vatican that he was to be granted a further audience. Pleased with Cardinal Bellarmino's support, he now looked forward to acquiring further approval from His Holiness personally. He knew in his heart that warnings and offers of support were both sirens that could see him shipwrecked and drowning in a needless debate with Church authorities, but he was confident of his political abilities.

He arrived at the great bronze doors of the Vatican feeling rather grand as he handed his letter of invitation over to the Swiss Guard. Even at a second viewing the sight before him was breathtaking, a colonnade and stairway appeared to stretch into infinity, with every step, column and lantern perfectly formed. A man appeared, as if from the marble itself, and spoke in the whisper demanded by the building. "Signor Galilei, please accompany me." They began the climb to infinity and Galileo's curiosity was immediately raised: he had not been taken by this route for his previous audience. He glanced back towards the entrance. The Swiss Guard now looked like a small a toy soldier.

Galileo felt the spring sun on his right shoulder as they walked along the loggia. The lustrous floor sent the sunlight into his eyes, blinding him to the Biblical scenes he passed under as they walked past a row of stone ancients.

The unctuous official proudly announced, "Signor Galilei, you are greatly honoured by His Holiness, he will be seeing you in one of his private rooms and not in the audience chamber." He paused, but Galileo remained silent as he could offer no insight as to why he was being treated to such an unusual honour. "In fact," he continued, "you will meet with His Holiness in the Stanza della Segnatura, His Holiness's personal study. I cannot recall His Holiness ever entertaining an audience in this office."

Galileo said nothing. He was now beginning to feel uncomfortable and wished only silence from the irritating man. They turned through the last door in the loggia and entered a large room, every surface of which was a work of art. He was struck by the slightly stale smell of a room that is not often used, but is regularly cleaned and polished. The whispering guide said something about Constantine and Raphael but Galileo was not listening. They passed through another, smaller, richly decorated room before entering a room with windows at either end; the room was dominated by two large frescoes that faced each other.

The pontiff sat on a gilt throne, slightly removed from a table and its accompanying plain chairs. Galileo crossed the floor and knelt at the feet of Pope Paul V, his lips lightly brushing the silken papal shoes. The pope gently placed his hands on Galileo's shoulders indicating he should stand, and with a little difficulty and creaking joints Galileo stood before the pope. The two men carried equally pugnacious features, and in another setting they might have been boxers squaring up for a fight.

"We welcome and bless the renowned mathematician and philosopher of the Medici court."

"Your Holiness, I beg to offer the humble greetings of their Most Serene Highnesses de Medici, for whom Holy

Mother Church is a constant source of inspiration and well being."

"Signor Galilei, we are honoured to meet again with our finest mathematician. We find it reassuring that this small land is, as the home of Holy Mother Church, the centre of the world for the faith and produces the world's finest minds, both theologians and natural philosophers, of course." Galileo should have been surprised at this effusion but he merely heard what he considered to be true, he gave no thought to the pontiff's reputation as a man with a dislike of intellectuals who were not theologians.

"Your Holiness is too kind. I am but a humble scholar and teacher."

"We all have much to learn in the eyes of God, and are always in need of good teachers."

"My two daughters at the Convent of San Matteo pray constantly for good will and wisdom in the world." Galileo decided to keep the conversation on solid Catholic ground and promote the good works and financial difficulties of the convent.

"You must be very proud to have made such a sacrifice for the greater good and Holy Mother Church." The pope spoke with practised appreciation.

"Yes, Your Holiness. Their devotion does much to strengthen my soul, and..."

The Pope interrupted Galileo before he could mention the good works of the Convent, and its need for extra income. "Yes, we understand that your soul may be in need of a little help, perhaps to be rescued from your mind?" Pope Paul decided he was going to enjoy his little cat and mouse game with the irksome mathematician. "Actually, it was your brilliant intellect that suggested to us that we should meet in this room." Pope Paul made an expansive gesture and rose to his feet. "We are, of course, aware of your discussions with Cardinal Bellarmino, and we thought to encourage you in your valuable work."

Galileo had been aware of the room's rich decoration but had not paid much attention to the frescoes. He looked past the pontiff and saw a fresco with two rows of figures separated by sky, the upper central figure he could see was Christ. The Pope glided past Galileo and stood before the fresco on the opposite wall, a bustling scene from antiquity.

"Signor Galilei, look closely at this fine work and you will see represented many of the ancient philosophers, whose works continue to influence much of our modern society. As you can see, the central two figures are Plato and Aristotle; note that Plato is pointing towards the sky, reminding us of the constant search for beauty and perfection beyond the physical world. By contrast, Aristotle is shown with his hand out thus, palm down, indicating the physical firmness of what can actually be experienced with our own senses."

Galileo was tempted to add, "If Aristotle could see what I have seen though my telescope he would agree with my observations", but kept the thought to himself.

"I am sure you will recognize this figure as Euclid," continued the Pope, moving towards the right-hand end of the fresco, "and just behind him we have Ptolemy with a model of the celestial spheres." Pope Paul fell silent and stepped back to admire the overall effect.

Galileo absorbed the scene thoughtfully, unsure whether or not the silence was an invitation to speak. He decided silence was the safest option and explored the image before him; the *trompe l'œil* was so well executed he wanted to climb the steps into the painting and walk amidst these flowers of knowledge. But a shadow began to draw across his appreciation when the message behind the pope's interest in the painting began to dawn on him.

His Holiness turned and crossed the room to the other fresco. Looking up at the two rows of figures, he declaimed, "Here we have the dispute over the Blessed Holy Sacrament. Below, on earth, are the thinkers and theologians and above, with our Lord, are the saints, prophets and kings. In short, this depiction shows the fundamental significance of the Holy Trinity and the triumph of spiritual Truth." He wheeled back across the room. "The toil, sweat and genius Signor Sanzio put into these wonderful images is as nothing compared to that which Holy Mother Church has put into reconciling these great pagan minds with Scripture." No further explanation was necessary for Galileo to appreciate the lesson: Holy Mother Church will not allow a mere mathematician to undermine the established order. Like many powerful men, the pope was enjoying his position as the arbiter of truth. "These are beautiful and thought provoking paintings, are they not?"

"Yes, Your Holiness. In fact, I would say that my eyes have been opened to a new light on the closeness between the great men of antiquity and Holy Mother Church."

Although Galileo's response was enough to inform Pope Paul that he had understood his thinly veiled message, the pope felt the need to make his point a little more forcefully. "Yes, of course, we are sure that Cardinal Bellarmino's letter clears up any possible areas of difficulty for you. Now tell me, you have spent some time in the beautiful city of Venice?" asked the pope enthusiastically.

This superficially innocent question unnerved Galileo. Relations between Rome and Venice were a running sore of ill feeling for the pontiff. "I was professor of mathematics at Padua University, and had occasion to visit Venice quite regularly."

"Tell me, did you meet the erudite Father Paolo Sarpi?"

This comes as a hammer blow: Galileo is taken back nine years to a bright autumnal day. A busy market day in Campo de le Becarie, just as he and Father Sarpi approach the Ponte de le Becarie he is grabbed from behind and pulled to the ground. He feels the hard cobbles meet his shoulder and elbow, his heart is racing as he attempts to struggle with the stranger, he doesn't have time to be afraid. Shock and surprise prevent him feeling any immediate pain. Suddenly aware of other shouts, Galileo realizes that Father Sarpi is also under attack. His attacker stops, seems to answer a call, gets up and runs away. There is a silent crowd just a few feet from Galileo. Another unknown hand helps him to his feet; he sees Paolo lying still, choking for breath, his head and torso are covered in blood. The ebony handle of a stiletto is protruding from his jaw. Horror and panic are kept at bay by the need to act. Drawing down his memories of medical school, Galileo searches Paolo for other wounds, mercifully there are none; he sends for some alcohol and clean linen, and removes the knife. After binding the wound, he has no difficulty finding help to carry Father Sarpi to Santa Maria Gloriosa. The would-be assassins having long since disappeared into the maze of alleys around Campo de le Becarie. A rumour that the attempt on Father Sarpi's life was ordered by the Vatican is around Venice as quickly as voices can travel.

Galileo's ears fill with the sound of his pounding heart, and he can feel Paolo's warm blood on his hands as he stands before the pontiff. It was thought by the Doge, and others of the ruling council, that this was almost certainly the work of the Vatican in an effort to silence Sarpi from speaking out against the papacy and counselling the Venetian state against agreeing to Vatican authority. He now looked at the man that probably gave the order for Sarpi's assassination, perhaps from within this very room. His dry mouth seized shut and his stomach turned over, filling his throat. He had to summon up all of his will power to reply calmly. "I, of course, met him at official functions, but could not claim to have known him well." He hated himself for denying his friendship with such a good and wise man, but it was the safest course of action. He did not pretend to have the strength and courage of Father Sarpi.

"Ah, well, no matter," replied Pope Paul, unconcerned by Galileo's poor lie. He had no real interest in Galileo's relationship with Sarpi, but he was assured by Galileo's ashen face that his message had been received. "We want you to know that you have our continued support in making use of this non-Scriptural hypothesis, that the earth revolves around the sun, if you must, in your own theorizing. No matter how great our knowledge of the physical world may be, or how accurate it may seem to be, the Glory of God will always be greater than man's understanding. We are all blind men in a maze which only the Lord can guide us through."

These words were of no comfort. "Thank you, Your Holiness..." Galileo was struggling to compose his next thought but the Pope spared him his difficulties.

"Alas, I am afraid that I must now attend to other business."

Galileo knelt, thanking the Pope for his valuable time, wisdom and support; his only thought was to get out as quickly as possible. The whispering official was waiting to guide him out. As they passed back through the adjoining room they walked past a fresco of a prison scene, the miracle of the liberation of Saint Peter. Had he noticed the painting it might have inspired him, or he might have recognized it as a symbol of the Pope's invincibility. He already knew that he was free only because the Pope willed it. The whispering official continued to talk about the building and its treasures but Galileo heard nothing. Before leaving the Vatican complex, Galileo made a critical decision: his life was worth more to him than his philosophy and he would never publish again.

6

Father Baccarini had been enjoying some candied orange blossoms and *pinocchiati* when Galileo came in to the Taverna Frascàti. His first reaction was to avoid being seen and leave but he quickly saw that Galileo was quite distracted; he watched the mathematician sit as far away from company as possible in a damp draughty corner of the taverna; he observed several people try to greet him but Galileo stared blindly ahead ignoring all attempts to engage him in conversation. Baccarini was sure that had Galileo sat directly opposite him he would not have noticed him. The Black Friar continued eating, his attention fixed on his former charge. In the midst of this noisy miscellany of commerce and joviality, there were two pools of quiet stillness: one desperate, the other curious. Baccarini had seen the look on Galileo's face before, in inquisitional proceedings. At the moment when the accused loses the light from his eyes he is ready to calmly accept whatever may befall him; but the Inquisitor was unsettled at seeing this look out of context. The longer he gazed at that isolated man, a personification of desperation, the greater the compassion he felt towards him. Father Baccarini's eyes began to sting, and he was sure one of the candied blossoms had caught the back of his throat. He left as unobtrusively as he had arrived.

By the time Galileo returned to Villa Medici the sun had made way for a shattered bowl of stars. He entered the main hall to be greeted by his friend Cardinal Barberini. His spirits began to lift. "Your Eminence, what a pleasant surprise."

"Leo, please let us not stand on ceremony." Cardinal Barberini spoke in mellifluous tones. His large eyes set in deep sockets contrasted with his sharply defined cheek-bones to give him the appearance of a solid and trustworthy man. Although only a few years younger than Galileo, he looked much younger.

"Your Eminence is too kind. Thank you, Maffeo, for such a generous gesture."

Galileo and Cardinal Barberini continued in this vein for some minutes, largely for the benefit of Galileo's host. It did no harm for Francesco to be reminded of the status of his guest. It was Caterina that uttered the inevitable question: "So, Leo," she asked brightly, "tell us all about your audience with His Holiness."

Galileo shrank inwardly at this enquiry but he did not want to disappoint Caterina, and so regurgitated as much information about the Vatican palace as he could recall from what the irritating attendant had told him. He said nothing of substance about the content of his audience but the presence of Maffeo and the attention of Caterina helped him animate his descriptions beyond what he actually felt. However, Galileo was sure he caught a flicker in Caterina's eye that suggested she was not convinced by his performance.

After a polite interval Galileo suggested to Maffeo that he join him on the roof terrace to observe the stars. "Let's see if you can discern Jupiter in the Milky Way, while the moon rides Sagittarius across what the Englishman Chaucer calls Watlynge Street."

The two men stepped out on to the roof terrace and Galileo immediately felt re-invigorated: "I love the smell of night air," he said, in the relaxed tone of a man that had just walked into his own home. A servant lit the brazier, whilst Galileo and Maffeo began manoeuvring a stand of about a metre and half high, with a heavy wooden base; they aligned the tray of the stand to the south. Galileo went back inside and returned with a metre-long tube covered in red leather and laid it in the tray of the stand. "Maffeo, I am so pleased with this new telescope. By making the eye-piece lens concave on both sides I have been able to almost double the magnification whilst making the tube almost half a metre shorter. I tell you, Venetian glass makers may be good but the Florentines are better; even so I finished these lenses myself, no amount of instruction will get the accuracy I require for clarity and magnification." He spoke enthusiastically for some time on the properties of different powders for grinding. The brazier was now in full glow. "You know, I am sure the key to finding longitude at sea lies in this tube and the stars. By the way, please don't let it be known that I made these lenses myself, it would not look good at court and I have enough trouble with some of those aristocratic fools."

"Of course not, Leo. Now, why are we really up here? It is always a joy to see the Lord's beautiful works so brilliantly displayed, but I suspect you had more than a lesson in optics in mind."

The sharp teeth of a gentle breeze bit at Galileo as he moved over to the brazier. "His Holiness was very charming and complimentary to me, and said nothing directly that was either unpleasant or threatening, but he packed a scorpion into his honeyed cake. I should have prepared myself for trouble when I realized that he was seeing me in one of his private apartments, the one that contains a fresco of Plato and Aristotle."

"The Stanza della Segnatura," Cardinal Barberini gently interjected. "His Holiness does nothing that could be described as coincidental."

"Oh, I am quite aware of that. His Holiness was quite explicit in reminding me of the importance to the

Church of the ancient philosophers, and that any modern views of the cosmos are anathema to Holy Mother Church. Then, out of nowhere, he asked me if I knew Father Paolo Sarpi."

"I see," uttered Maffeo gently. The rumour and received wisdom of the upper echelons of the Vatican authorities was that the attempt on Father Sarpi's life had indeed been instigated by the Holy See. Although Cardinal Barberini had not engaged in such damaging gossip he was in no doubt that the Pope's reference to Sarpi could only be interpreted as a threat to Galileo. The two men stood in silence, the brazier lighting their faces in a haunting red glow. Time seemed to stop within the orange-yellow world of the brazier, until eventually Maffeo spoke. "His Holiness made no other comment on you being able to discuss Copernican hypothesis?"

"No, other than again asserting that I am free to do only that. But it was clear to me that any discussion of the earth moving about the sun, even as a hypothesis, will be open to scrutiny. I think we can both see that His Holiness intends to silence me and he has succeeded." Galileo was shouting, crying out plaintively. "It will be far too dangerous for me to pursue this subject. Let us not forget that Pope Clement had no qualms about burning Giordano Bruno, another supporter of the Copernican view, and no pontiff has ever undermined the decisions of a predecessor."

"Leo, please, let us not get carried away. His Holiness obviously cannot openly support your views. As you say, the Congregation of the Index has already passed verdict on Copernicus, but did not Cardinal Bellarmino provide you with a certificate stating that you had not been summoned by the Inquisition? I can assure you, if His Holiness considered you to be a heretic you would already be in chains in Castel Sant' Angelo."

"Or banished into exile like Foscarini. Now that the Index has banned his book, heaven only knows what will happen to him."

The Cardinal's lips moved, barely perceptively, in a considered but rejected response. This slight movement was, however, accentuated by the sharp shadows of the brazier and Galileo noticed this unborn thought. "What? What have you heard about Foscarini?"

Slowly and reluctantly Barberini replied. "We received news this morning, from the monastery at Montalto, that Father Foscarini died of a fever four days ago."

"No..." Galileo exhaled this single word as he leaned back on to the wall of the terrace, retching. Barberini put a consoling arm about him.

"I am sorry, I did not know you were friends."

"I never actually met the good Father, but we corresponded and were philosophical brothers. I am next."

"Nonsense. Father Foscarini died of natural causes, and I am sure that if there were any plot against your life we would have known about it by now." The Cardinal's voice lacked conviction. "It was ill advised of Foscarini to argue for an alternative interpretation of Scripture. He knew that no individual may interpret Scripture contrary to the common agreement of the Church Fathers. Not even His Holiness may take such a step, only the Councils of Holy Mother Church have the authority to interpret Scripture. Perhaps his unfortunate but, I am sure, natural death was a blessing to him and Holy Mother Church. His Holiness would not have wished matters worse for either the Church or Foscarini by holding a public trial." The cardinal's voice trailed off, he seemed to realize that his words sounded like a rationale for killing Father Foscarini.

"So Foscarini's good luck was Bruno's ill fortune," snapped Galileo. "How long did Bruno languish in Castel Sant' Angelo before meeting the fire? Was it five, six, seven years? Should I leap off the terrace now? Tell me, Your Eminence, according to some interpretations of *Joshua* the sun moves about the earth, and thus this is a matter of Scriptural truth and faith. Is this also the case, as it says in *Tobit*, that the Archangel Raphael had a dog?"

Cardinal Barberini's response was swift and sharp. "Do not trifle with the Word of our Lord, and expect salvation. Now," Maffeo removed the steel from his voice, "calm yourself, Leo, you are neither an apostate madman like Bruno, nor a fool like Foscarini. The way is still open for you to use Copernicus for celestial calculations, though I think you would be wise to adopt the hypothetical model of Tycho Brae."

Reeling from the cardinal's flash of anger, Galileo spoke with heartfelt humility. "I am sorry. But, ingenious as Tycho's calculations are, he still places the earth at the centre of the universe and I am certain that is physically wrong. I do appreciate the difference between natural truth and the Truth of Revelation, like Foscarini, I believe it to be in the interests of Holy Mother Church not to close the door on this debate. However, no matter what I may think, the Index has drawn its conclusions and I have to live by them. How do you think Duke Cosimo is going to take the news from the Index? I fear that I am finished at court."

"How can you say that?" Maffeo spoke gently, wrapping Galileo in the soft timbre of his voice. "You are a brilliant mathematician and philosopher, with many inventions and observations to your name."

"I have spent my whole life taking measurements, making observations and turning them into philosophical principles; at the same time making sure I get to know the right people to advance my position. Until, finally, I discover the stars around Jupiter, but it was not this observation, nor its interpretation, that found me a place at court; what earned me my place there was my gift of this finding to the Medicis. I don't believe Duke Cosimo has any real interest in astronomy or the nature of the universe, but he is very interested in astrology and the divinatory support the Medician stars offer him for his sense of family history and, more importantly, his right to power. The Duke has supported me, and my espousal of the view that the earth moves around the sun. I cannot alter my position without embarrassing Duke Cosimo. So you see, I am finished." Galileo paused to breathe in the warm air of the brazier. "One day, mathematics and observation will describe the universe and all of its worlds and their natures, and it saddens me greatly that Holy Mother Church will rue that day. As the great poet says:

> *Everything that is created*
> *Is part of a mutual order, and that is the shape*
> *Which makes the universe resemble God.*

"I know, and I do understand. But we have to have faith that our Lord will one day provide the occasion for you to be right in public. Times and people change, even ideas may change but something that is physically wrong can never be right. So try to be patient and careful." Maffeo once more wrapped Galileo in his soft voice. The world of the brazier had all but disappeared when they returned inside.

7

Ludovico delle Colombe was not sure why Cardinal Bellarmino had asked him to visit, but he imagined it would be something to do with Galileo. It was certainly a great honour to be invited to the home of the cardinal and so it was with some trepidation that he waited to be announced to the great and learned man. "Signor delle Colombe, Your Eminence."

"Thank you, Giuseppe." The cardinal was out of Ludovico's line of sight and the hoarse fragile voice that spoke could have been that of the building itself. "And please bring us some wine." Ludovico was shown into the main hall of the palazzo and, despite the warm sunlight flowing into the room, Bellarmino sat on a couch with a blanket wrapped around his legs, the embers of a fire still glowing. A broad shaft of sunlight lit the cardinal in a halo of dust: he looked every inch the saintly being he aspired to be. But even in the glow of late summer he appeared pallid, like wet stucco. Ludovico had to kneel in the bright beam to touch his lips to the blue stone offered to him by a marble hand.

"Signor delle Colombe, please sit down."

"I am deeply honoured by Your Eminence." Ludovico sat a little awkwardly in the small chair opposite Bellarmino, and gazed at the elderly cardinal in polite expectation. The frail eminence hurried past the pleasantries.

"Thank you for responding to an old man's request for company so promptly. I did not expect you to be in Rome this year, how long will you be staying?"

"I shall be returning to Florence in two or three weeks."

"Ah, Florence. It has been more years than I care to recall since I last visited our fair Tuscany." Bellarmino was not usually a wistful man, but the conspiratorial air of "our fair Tuscany" helped put Ludovico at his ease. "Now tell me, have there been any interesting developments at the Academy?"

"The debates surrounding the comets that appeared two years ago still rage, without satisfactory conclusion. But I am sure your eminence is already aware of this from the fine scholars of the Collegio Romano." Ludovico now knew that this was indeed to be a meeting about Galileo. A look of mutual understanding flashed between the two men.

"I dare say that Signor Galilei has been making his presence felt in this astronomical debate."

"He has not voiced his views directly but through the agency of one of his acolytes, a certain Mario Guiducci."

"I see. And are his views, as far as one may tell through this other organ, any more palatable than they had previously been?"

"Indeed not, Your Eminence."

"I see. Are you and Signor Galilei still in disagreement about the place of the sun?"

Giuseppe entered with the wine, creating a pause long enough for Ludovico to decide that Bellarmino's position had not changed since the Galileo business of five years ago. News, gossip and rumours about Galileo's discussions with the esteemed cardinal were still circulating in Florence. "As Your Eminence is already aware, Signor Galilei is a mere mathematician who seems to believe that the tradesman's skill in laying bricks may be compared to the artistry and vision of the architect. Despite his endless attempts to prove arguments with home-made toys and numbers, he is incapable of seeing, let alone accepting, that the fine argument of discursive philosophy cannot be reduced to the simple bricks and mortar of numbers. Mathematics is inadequate to describe the universe, since mathematics is a mere abstraction of the Lord's work."

"Quite so," agreed the cardinal encouragingly.

"There is also the great risk that his mathematics may predict things which do not exist, or are impossible in nature. To accept the views of Signor Galilei I would have to turn my back on the greatest philosophers and theologians of more than a thousand years, as well as the findings of the Congregation of the Index. If I were to agree with the Copernican heresy, for even a moment, I would be consigning all of my work, my faith and my fellow scholars to eternal damnation. No, I do not, cannot, and will not concur with the views of Galileo; he will feed the hounds of hell with his blasphemous arrogance." Ludovico took some wine at Bellarmino's gestured invitation, leaned back into the chair and awaited the cardinal's response.

"I am aware of your fine work as a bulwark against those that would attempt to undermine the writing of the great Aristotle. Indeed I enjoyed your response to Signor Galilei's discourse on why bodies float; yes, it is a fine evocation of the Aristotelian position in answer to Galileo's collection of tricks with toys. I was re-reading your work again recently and was pleasantly surprised to note that even before we in the Collegio Romano became aware of Galileo's views of the universe you drew out his association with the Copernican theory. But that was all some years ago now, tell me why has your pen remained still for so long since then?"

Ludovico drew a long breath. "The perspicacity of Your Eminence has touched my very heart on this matter. If you will indulge me I will outline the two chief reasons for my recent silence. Signor Galilei has the support of the

Grand Duke; such a patron guarantees sales of any publication and therefore reduces the potential risk to those wishing to offer financial support in the production of a pamphlet or book. I, however, did have the support of the noble but less eminent Signor Giovanni Medici; despite the clear and fine nobility of his Excellency, his name does not garner the required financial support for publication. Furthermore, my defence of the Aristotelian position on why objects float was a direct response to that published by Signor Galilei; both works owe their origins to a feast given by the Grand Duke at the villa of Signor Salviati. As you can imagine, those present represented the finest nobility and intelligentsia of the Florentine republic. The Duke invited Signor Galilei and me to debate the matter of why some objects should float and others not. As is his wont, Galilei chose not to argue the matter philosophically but rather to amuse his audience by insulting and humiliating me. Being greatly amused by his performance, the Grand Duke invited Signor Galilei to publish his argument. His Excellency Giovanni Medici, however, was persuaded by my presentation of the Aristotelian position and supported the publication of my response to Galileo's treatise on floating bodies. However, since that publication I have not been able to acquire sufficient financial support for any other publications."

Cardinal Bellamrnio was consoling. "Ah, fickle are the ways of princes. This is a great pity, the world and Holy Mother Church require good souls, such as yourself, to explain the philosophical intricacies of the Ancients to a wide audience and in accordance with Scripture. I know that you have suffered harsh and public insults from Signor Galilei, and that many of your fellow scholars have also been made to look fools by his merciless tongue. I am greatly disturbed and saddened that one man appears capable of shaming our scholastic institutions, and creating such disharmony between wise and intelligent men."

Ludovico nodded, appreciative of the cardinal's concern but also troubled by Bellarmino's description of the situation. Delle Colombe had been involved in numerous debates with Signor Galilei, and whilst being aware of the wider impression of Galileo's impact he had always been too preoccupied with the philosophical details and his personal animosity towards his opponent to see the greater implications of Galileo's arguments. But Ludovico now began to see Cardinal Bellarmino's wider concern. "I am afraid that there are many self-proclaimed intellectuals that side with Galileo and he thus brings scholar into conflict with scholar. Indeed, I believe he threatens the stability and reputation of our universities."

Bellarmino's tone was grave and measured. "I fear that the influence of Signor Galilei may have repercussions far beyond that of university professors, Signor delle Colombe. I know you to be a true and faithful servant of Holy Mother Church, but I must press you for your word that this conversation will remain absolutely confidential."

Ludovico replied without hesitation. "Of course, Your Eminence. My soul is guided by your wisdom and trust." Feeling emboldened by his new role as ecclesiastical confident, Ludovico asked, "But, if I may be so bold, Your Eminence, why was it that Galileo was not subjected to the full power and authority of the Congregation of the Inquisition when the opportunity presented itself five years ago? His position has not actually differed since he was last in Rome."

"You must understand, Signor delle Colombe, that we live in a world in which questions of right, wrong, truth, justice, beauty and so on, are determined not by observation or philosophizing, as you might reasonably assume, but by patronage. In short, the breadth and depth of the economic and political power of Signor Galilei's supporters, to which you have already alluded, was such that Holy Mother Church could not risk placing excessive tension on some delicate relationships. Contrary to the teachings of our Lord, influence and power are still clothed as a rich man; we live in a world in which a diabolic pact between wealth and power rules absolutely, the damnable consequence of every mortal soul that ever craved that to which he had no right. I pray that God may forgive my failure in effecting any change in such attitudes."

Bellarmino drifted off into his thoughts. Ludovico was not sure that he should comment on the Cardinal's *ubi sunt* beyond a mumbled and vague agreement. "Your Eminence is, as always, able to see to the very core of the vile and corrupt soul of man and this must surely be a cause for great sadness and pain."

"Indeed it is. There are times when I wonder if Signor Galilei is actually doing the work of our Lord by trying to shake us from the comfortable torpor that inevitably leads to corruption. But then I remind myself that our Lord was a teacher, and if the very foundations of our educational establishments are rent asunder it will do unimaginable harm. It is inconceivable to me that He could wish to see the great works of our forefathers destroyed by a single man." The sunlight had now moved off Bellarmino and they sat in comparative gloom with only a small corner of the room illumined by the heavenly shaft.

"I hope you will forgive my asking this, Your Eminence, but why have you chosen to discuss this grave matter with me rather than one of your esteemed colleagues?"

A deep creaking sigh passed across the stone lips of the Cardinal. "I believe you are a man who not only understands but can also counter Signor Galilei's arguments with firmly resolute Aristotelian debate; also you are in a position to fully appreciate the potential harm he is capable of doing to scholars and universities. Moreover, and it breaks my heart to say this, some of my fellow shepherds are supporters of Galilei although I am sure that this is not the case for the majority; there are even some who are too concerned about their own naked ambitions to risk getting embroiled in this business. So, I hope I can rely on your help in securing the future of our authoritative teachings?"

"Of course, Your Eminence, but I am not sure what more I can do. As you know, I argue against Galileo at every opportunity, and though I am usually repaid with some humiliating quip from his common tongue I shall never stop challenging him."

"I certainly appreciate the good work that you put your great learning to in dealing with Signor Galilei, and will give you what support and succour I may whilst I live. But let us be honest, I am an old man and I feel death settling in my eyes; this battle, for that is what it is, will outlast me. I would like us to consider the future and how to protect it against these wild and dangerous heresies."

Ludovico was at a loss as to how to respond to the overwhelming responsibility placed before him. He watched the marble hand of the Cardinal slowly and deliberately raise his glass to his stony lips. Bellarmino's frailty was clearly apparent.

After dabbing away a spot of moisture from his mouth, Bellarmino continued. "Try as we might, we cannot control the future for something unexpected always occurs." Bellarmino sighed with a faint laugh. "The best we can hope to do is influence what may happen, pray that we are right and that right will triumph. Remember that certainty exists only with God, and so a certain man is certainly blasphemous." He paused before returning his focus to Ludovico. "You say that Signor Galilei has been silent on the subject of the sun of late?"

"Yes, Your Eminence. I do not believe I have heard any pronouncements, from him personally, about his stationary sun theory since he was last in Rome."

"Good. If this remains the case then there will be little for you to do, unless one of these other voices he employs is fool enough to give him to us. However, times change, and pontiffs with them, and who can tell what empty-headed modern notions may be employed in the future to aid someone's personal glory? In addition to your intellect and skill as a philosopher, you have a further important advantage over Signor Galilei." Ludovico stared in disbelief at what previously unknown hidden powers the cardinal might reveal to him. Bellarmino continued without attempting to disguise the contempt in his voice. "This mathematician is a man of vulgar stock that has worked his way into courtly circles, he does not have the innate knowledge required to appreciate the fine gradations of etiquette necessary to operate successfully as a courtier. His mind cannot control his mouth, so his own words are his worst enemy; these will make him vulnerable in time." The marble hand reached again for the glass.

"I am deeply moved that you should consider me for such an important role, Your Eminence, but I still do not see how I am to succeed. I am sorry to say that Galileo usually manages to garner sufficient support to gain the upper hand on me." Ludovico spoke without complaint.

"I appreciate your candour and concern, but let me assure you that I do not intend to entrust this role to you alone. I say this not because I doubt your abilities but because I believe that two horses and two riders are required for this game. Do you know the master of Santa Maria sopra Minerva, Father Thomaso Caccini?"

"I have met him once or twice and, of course, I am aware of his sermons." The cardinal's plan was now falling into place for Ludovico.

"Quite so, you and he share a single vision, but from differing viewpoints, of Signor Galilei. When the time comes, your Florentine connections and learning may be harnessed with Father Caccini's experience to, how shall I put this? Create a resolution between the long-held views of the sacred and profane authorities, and the modern fancies followed by those that lack the proper vision."

"When did you envisage that Father Caccini and I should begin this action?" asked Ludovico nervously.

"When?" Bellarmino's face broke into a knowing smile. "Why, when the time is right of course. I am sure that between the two of you the right time will make itself known. I shall write you a letter of introduction to Father Caccini."

Bellarmino reached for his writing materials on the couch next to him and, leaning on a writing board, drafted a letter in the angular, irregular scrawl of the elderly and infirm.

Ludovico was not inspired by Bellarmino's response, but could see that there was no point in pursuing the cardinal. He just hoped that Bellarmino had already held a similar discussion with Caccini. If he had not, how receptive was Caccini going to be to him and were there any risks to himself in opening this discussion with Caccini? "Your Eminence, would it be rude of me to ask if you have already spoken to Father Caccini on this matter?"

"No, of course not. I have spoken with Father Caccini on many occasions," replied Bellarmino without looking up from his letter.

8

Insects, infections and a merciless sun tortured Rome. Ludovico sat inside the cool quiet of the Pantheon; he liked to come here to contemplate the architectural purity of a sphere within a cylinder. The building was, for him, a physical representation of Aristotle's pronouncement of the immutability of the sphere and the perfection of the circle. He sat admiring a beam of Godliness pouring through the oculus of this paragon of pagan thought and design. Ludovico's spirits were lifted by the sight of the new buildings finally under construction in the area, for it had always upset him that such a philosophically important structure should be in a run-down and squalid part of the city. Any doubts he had about meeting Father Caccini dissipated with the growing certainty that the task before him was right, just and true. As he gathered his thoughts before leaving, he stood for a moment under the muscular bronze beams of the portico, letting his eyes adjust to the full glare of daylight before walking around the corner to Santa Maria sopra Minerva.

The contrast between the simple sphere, so admired by Ludovico, and the long vaulted nave of Santa Maria with its azure sky and marble columns could hardly be greater. After genuflecting before the altar he approached a young Dominican who directed him to a door at the end of the transept, a modest portal linking the church to the offices of the Dominican Order. Father Caccini greeted him enthusiastically, "Signor delle Colombe, what a pleasure to meet you again."

"The pleasure is all mine, Father," said Ludovico, feeling a little embarrassed by the force of Caccini's cordiality and overly firm handshake. "His Eminence Cardinal Bellarmino suggested that I visit you; I believe he explains his reasons in this letter." He passed the letter to Caccini, regretting not having had the courage to break the seal himself. Father Caccini barely glanced at the letter before slapping it down on his desk with a self-satisfied "Good. I've been expecting you." Smiling broadly as he straightened up, he continued, "In these difficult days Holy Mother Church seems always to be in need of faithful and loyal defenders. Perhaps we should go somewhere a little more comfortable to talk?"

"As you wish," replied Ludovico cautiously.

After a carriage ride of some fifteen or twenty minutes Father Caccini ordered his driver to stop and await their return. In the lazy warmth of late afternoon the two men walked through the quarry of antique stone that was once Circus Maximus. Father Caccini began speaking, as much to an unseen congregation as to Ludovico. "I love to come here when I want to think and be away from the busy ears and tongues of the city. I find this place such an inspiration: we have death, blood, the race and the competition that is life in this bloody pagan arena. But then there is the promise of salvation and re-birth in our modern churches built from the very stones of this deathly arena. More importantly though, should anyone overhear our conversation it is very likely they will be either too drunk or ignorant to understand its import."

Ludovico could see the need for circumspection but his nostrils felt defiled by the overwhelming scent of humanity in this awful place; he considered Caccini's imagery a little overplayed for a man-made quarry. Father Caccini settled into a possessive stride as they walked. "So, His Eminence Cardinal Bellarmino has chosen you to aid me in the matter of the universe?"

Ludovico immediately prickled at the servile role implied by Father Caccini. "I think His Eminence envisaged a union of minds."

Father Caccini responded with due courtesy. "Of course, please accept my apologies; it was not my intention to slight you. I trust that you will understand my frustration at fighting that man's heresies for such a long time."

"Yes. I too have felt the sharp and withering tongue of the arrogant heretic."

"You know Signor Galilei well?"

Ludovico felt a bond beginning to develop with Father Caccini; they were indeed of a like mind. "Socially, not at all. Intellectually, very well indeed. You might say we represent opposite sides of a coin. We are both members of the Florentine Academy: I debate philosophical points using the discursive techniques and works of the finest minds the world has ever known, whereas Signor Galilei spends his time devising methods for trying to make the great minds of the Ancients appear foolish. He appears to have a particular dislike for Aristotle. He uses neither the language nor techniques of proper philosophical debate, he writes in the common tongue and argues from positions of his own devising. And, of course, he seems to take great delight in trying to make me appear a complete fool whenever the opportunity presents itself. Fortunately my colleagues and other members of the Academy are, by and large, able to see him for the blasphemous false prophet he is."

They exchanged Galileo stories for more than an hour, as their feet picked a route through the spoils of the ghostly arena.

Eventually, Father Caccini suggested the outline of a plan. "His Eminence Cardinal Bellarmino is without doubt the wisest of men; although Galileo has been silent for the past few years he suspects it will not last. There is little we can do in relation to the last warning given to Galileo and so we must wait until he makes some new public pronouncements." Father Caccini did not waste this opportunity to show off his intimate knowledge of the inner workings of the Inquisition and Cardinal Bellarmino's dealings with Galileo. "I am sure you will be constantly alert to Galileo's work, teachings and even his discussions at the Florentine Academy. Should he utter anything at all that appears theologically questionable, contact me directly, rather than the Inquisitional Office in Florence. When the time is ripe, we will have to be certain of ensuring a solid case is built against him. Naturally, we will also have to be careful in our correspondence, lest it fall into the waters of Galilee."

"Yes, indeed, I think it would be safer for us not to communicate unless absolutely necessary, so as not to arouse any suspicions," replied Ludovico enthusiastically.

II

1
1624

By the time the spring rains had stopped, and it was possible to travel again, Galileo had become so irascible and ill tempered that his household was more than happy to see him set off for Acquasparta. He had received invitations to stay with Prince Cesi, at his country home; from there he would continue on to Rome and an audience with Pope Urban VIII. During the course of the winter his excitement and impatience to set off on this honour filled journey drove him, and anyone near him, close to madness.

Despite the cold weather Galileo sat up with his driver for both days of their journey. Brimming over with energy and a desire to talk, he lectured the driver at length on the important publications of the Lincean academy on botany, zoology, geology and his own contributions to astronomy; he spoke reverently of its great and wise membership and their wonderfully farsighted founder and patron Prince Federico Cesi. He assaulted the driver's ears with stories of the Cesi family, the greatness of Prince Cesi and the dispute between father and son over the establishment of an organization that the Duke considered to be money wasted on nonsense. In his excitement, and lacking any discretion, he even spoke of the rumours that the Duke of Acquasparta was quite mad. The chagrin of the driver was only increased by the inability of the rough road, the sharp-edged showers or the cold wind to silence Galileo; at journey's end, the driver did not seem convinced that this trip had been such a great honour.

During the weeks that Galileo stayed at Palazzo Cesi he felt himself to be in perfect harmony with his surroundings, his company and his thoughts. He spent evenings observing the night sky and conversing with Prince Cesi and his fellow scholars in this elite community of great minds. At supper one evening, Dr Johann-Baptist Winther related his first impressions and feelings upon arriving at Palazzo Cesi.

The physician cleared his throat noisily and stood with glass in hand directed to the prince. "Most honoured Prince and noble host, upon arriving I was entranced by the sight of this great palace, along with the sheer loveliness of the green and fertile meadows lying beneath it, terminated by the most beautiful mountains. It seemed at first sight, to resemble nothing more than those Elysian fields celebrated by the poets; or the celestial gardens whose beauty no mortal painter, with whatever skilled mixture of colours, could ever attain."

Galileo listened with approval and joined the applause that rumbled around the table. Prince Cesi, small and delicately featured with something of the look of a naughty child, modestly accepted the compliment. "You are most kind, Johann, indeed I am grateful to you all, wise and brilliant men each of you." At this there was uproar around the table as the guests loudly vied with each other in protesting their ignorance, humility and gratitude to Prince Cesi.

In his last week at Palazzo Cesi Galileo received sorrowful news that brought a brooding darkness over his halcyon retreat. Prince Cesi invited him to join him in his private quarters to break the news. "My dear Leo, news has reached me that I know will be a cause of great sorrow to you." His voice creaked as he spoke; Galileo remained silent, he saw that the Prince's face had lost its boyish look and knew this would indeed be bad news.

Federico continued, "Leo, it seems that the Lord has appointed me to pass on this grave news. Your friend and dedicatee, our fellow Lincean, Monsignor Cesarini has left this world to sit with our Lord in Heaven."

Galileo's eyes filled and his voice creaked. When? Where? How? These questions filtered briefly through his mind but did not pass his lips. He was vaguely aware of the prince's voice passing on condolences and concerns about the loss of a key Vatican ally in the shape of the chamberlain to His Holiness, but Galileo stood and left the room in silence without taking his leave.

It was some days before Galileo saw or spoke to anyone, and with his time in Palazzo Cesi coming to an end, he began to look forward to travelling to Rome. His mood improved considerably when he was told that the prince had planned a great feast in his honour for his last night at the Palazzo.

The feast was not a disappointment to Galileo, the renown of the Cesi family and the Lincean Academy would bring guests from Rome and Florence. Amongst the assembled wealth and greatness, Galileo was particularly pleased to see Cardinal Orsini, His Eminence had provided staunch support to Galileo during his previous difficulties in Rome. Fellow Lincean, Giovanni Ciàmpoli, had taken the trouble to travel from Rome at relatively short notice, and he, as private secretary to the Pontiff, was a comrade of some significance. Galileo could not believe his luck when his friend, Cardinal Maffeo Barberini, was elected pontiff and acceded to the papal throne as Urban VIII. As if that were not enough good fortune, Urban then appointed Giovanni as his private secretary.

As the guests renewed old acquaintances and made new ones, all whilst trying not to be obvious in attempting to gain the prince's attention, Prince Cesi guided Galileo and Giovanni away from the main concentration of discussion on the pretext of showing off some rather dull corner seats he had commissioned for the Lincean Academy. The seats were not particularly impressive. Designed to hold two people in discussion, they were squat and dark with a utilitarian appearance, their backs decorated with the Lynx emblem of the academy. After a cursory examination, with perfunctory and unconvincing noises of appreciation from Giovanni, the Prince indicated that the two men be seated. Although not usually politically astute Galileo knew enough to let the prince lead the conversation.

"Giovanni, it is true, is it not, that you have the ear of His Holiness?"

"Yes indeed, Your Highness."

"And do you know his mind on certain matters?"

Giovanni replied with proud certainty, moving his gaze between Galileo and the prince. "I believe, Your Highness, that my mind is entirely in harmony with that of His Holiness."

"I think we are both aware," Prince Cesi continued, "that Leo has not yet written the book he is bursting to pen. What would be the position of our modern-thinking Pontiff to a proposal that Leo actually write the work that has remained locked within him these years?"

Giovanni replied with deliberation, without attempting to conceal his enjoyment of this time with the prince. "Your Highness, the minds of Leo, His Holiness and myself are as alike as three different glasses, each of which contains wine of the same grape: differing vessels but only one taste." Giovanni sat back and puffed slightly at the ingenuity of his allusion. Grinning broadly, Galileo reached out his hand onto Giovanni's shoulder and thanked him warmly.

"Excellent!" Declaimed Prince Cesi. "So the Lincean Academy can look forward to publishing Leo's next work with Vatican approval?"

Giovanni nodded sagely, and they all returned to the main throng of guests.

Galileo was introduced to Father Niccolò Riccardi by Giovanni; after the customary salutations Giovanni said, "Leo, old friend, Father Riccardi has not only had a recent promotion within the Curia, but he is also the cousin of Caterina Niccolini, wife of the Florentine Ambassador."

"My goodness, what a coincidence, I know them well and hope to be receiving their fine hospitality when I return to Rome. I trust they are both well?" asked Galileo warmly.

Father Riccardi, a giant of a man, as wide as he was tall, responded with a booming voice. "Oh, they are both in very fine health and I happen to know that they are looking forward to your visit."

"Thank you, your are most gracious."

"Father Riccardi," interjected Giovanni, "I wonder if you would be kind enough to remind me of the detail of your promotion?"

It was with seemingly genuine, if loud, humility that the Father replied. "My promotion is but a small advancement to a lowly post in the Sacred Palace." In a loud whisper, he added, "A rather dull position licensing books."

The conversation flowed throughout the evening, ranging widely across politics, philosophy, religion, literature, but remained a tactful distance from the place of the sun. Prince Cesi, with consummate ease, brought the gathering together.

"Nobles, friends. This evening we celebrate the great works completed and yet to be written by our honourable and brilliant friend Galileo Galilei, and to wish him well for his journey to Rome." The sound of approval circled the room, and the prince let the moment breathe before continuing. "Our eponymous Argonaut Lynceus was said to have been so sharp-sighted that he could see to the centre of the earth.

Today, thanks to Signor Galilei, we can look further than that to the stars. And I believe that we are on the cusp of entering into a new phase of thinking and discovery, which will surely have the approval of His Holiness himself. We face a new era, friends, with the old one firmly behind us." The prince raised his glass and roared, "Galileo Galilei!" The room reverberated with shouts of agreement and approval.

Honoured and emboldened by wine, food and good cheer, Galileo addressed the assembled guests. "My honourable and noble host, Your Most Serene Majesty Prince Cesi, Your Eminence, friends, please raise your glasses. Now hold your glass to the light a moment and admire the beauty of this red moisture held together by light and dedicate it to the honour of His Beatitude Pope Urban the Eighth, a modern man for modern times." A cheer rang out. "Friends, almost a decade has passed since my last visit to Rome. Then, I left that fine city feeling despondent and resigned to a life of quiet teaching and engineering" – a fond chuckle circulated the room, as none of the guests had ever known Leo to be "quiet" – "or perhaps even taking up my father's trade of musician." He put his glass on to the table. "I felt certain that I was to be silenced forever and could never have dreamed of an evening such as this when, despite the efforts of certain members of the Collegio Romano, His Holiness has seen fit to support me by offering me an audience to discuss my returning to an examination of the heavens and the employment of the Copernican hypothesis. Tomorrow I leave this Palazzo inspired by the great wisdom of His Holiness, may the Lord bless him with a long life. In our rapidly changing world we must not allow our perceptions to be dulled by blind doctrine; this is a time of possibilities, in which our minds should be free of the prison of dogmatic adherence to the authority of the ancients. Allow your vision to shine and cast light on our dark ignorance of the world." Toning down his triumphalism to a sombre reverence, he continued, "We can never know the mind of Almighty God, but He has given us vision and intelligence with which to appreciate more fully the wonder of His works. Only with detailed observation and measurement, in short, mathematics, can we hope to even begin to understand the smallest speck of His creation."

Prince Cesi led the applause with heartfelt gusto. "Tomorrow, Leo will set off along the Via Flaminia for Rome and each step that he takes will bring us closer to the future."

***

"You are free to make use of Copernicus's theory of the earth's motion about the sun, in purely hypothetical terms of course. However, you must not use this theory in your discussions about the causes of the tides. Philosophers of your calibre should be encouraged in your work to continue to produce books as stimulating as *The Assayer*." His Holiness, Pope Urban VIII, spoke with mock firmness. But Galileo knew only too well that Urban's reference to the causes of the tides was not meant in jest; he nevertheless hid his disappointment convincingly. Whilst the Copernican theory remained a prohibited if not quite a heretical hypothesis, Galileo could not see how he could resume his work to explain the movement of the tides: he was certain that as the earth moved so the bodies of water upon it also moved, like water in a jug. Urban made no secret of his knowledge of Galileo's thoughts on this matter but clearly would not risk a hypothesis being proved that could undermine the authority of Aristotle and thus jeopardize the primacy of Holy Mother Church in the interpretation of Scripture.

Galileo misjudged the depth of support he might expect from his old friend. "Your Holiness is, as always, gracious, kind and wise. But I wonder if I might just press Your Beatitude a little further? In order to defend herself against possible future misinterpretations, perhaps Holy Mother Church could at least formally accept the Copernican theory as a hypothetical possibility."

Urban's pleasant and engaging countenance immediately changed to an implacable visage, the warmth of his voice disappeared.

"The diabolic war in the north has drained our blood for longer than could have been imagined." His eyes hardened as he spoke. "Indeed, it has become a ravenous beast that feeds relentlessly on lives, souls and money. But we continue to feed this beast because we are responsible for maintaining the primacy of Holy Mother Church against her enemies, the pretenders to her absolute authority in Scriptural exegesis. You," said Urban with a pointed emphasis, "should consider more directly the lives expended on this venture for it is minds such as yours that advance our technologies so that we may dispatch our enemies more efficiently. Though it is a matter of some regret to us that you have considered your pockets over the lives of our fine soldiers, because our enemies are now able to fire their cannon as accurately as us." Pope Urban paused distractedly. "Holy Mother Church must be defended, the blood on my hands is the blood of martyrs; never forget that my sanguineous signature is no less stained than your inventiveness."

Galileo the colour drain from his face, His Holiness was right, he had sold his ranging device to anyone that wanted to buy one with no thought to the implications for his countrymen. As he now considered the costly visceral effectiveness of his military compass, he stood before the Pope, humbled and ashamed.

"But let us not part with ill humour." The Pope's voice resumed its warm conversational tone. "Giovanni! If you please." Giovanni left his desk and brought a small parcel to the pontiff. "Thank you. Signor Galilei, we are proud to honour our famed mathematician and philosopher to the Medici Court with this Pontifical medal as a small token of our gratitude to your fine works."

Galileo was genuinely surprised and taken quite off balance at this sudden change of mood and demonstration of affection; he still had the image of dead and bloodied soldiers

77

in his mind. He bowed his head slightly and Pope Urban placed the ribbon of the medal on his shoulders.

"Your Holiness, I am speechless at this fine gesture of love."

"I have also arranged a pension of sixty crowns for your son Vincenzio. It is but a small amount and thus requires but little work for the Church in Florence."

"Your Holiness, I am overwhelmed with gratitude."

"Finally, please deliver this, our greetings, to Her Most Serene and Excellent Highness Duchess Christina."

"Of course, Your Holiness, it shall be my first duty upon my return to Florence."

The audience over, Galileo was escorted from the palace by the Pope's private secretary Giovanni. As they passed through the antechamber, Giovanni spoke briefly with a young man. "His Holiness will see you presently, Signor Bernini, please be patient."

They went out onto the loggia and Galileo addressed the secretary. "Please convey to His Holiness my abject apologies. It was indeed selfish of me to press him when he has been so kind."

"Don't worry, Leo, he hasn't forgotten your friendship. I will make sure that the order is drawn up for a Franciscan Visitator to attend to the sisters of San Matteo. You can assure your daughter that the flock will receive a good shepherd."

"Thank you. Virginia and her fellow sisters will keep you in their prayers for arranging a Father for them."

"I think, Leo, you mean Suor Maria Celeste."

"Yes, of course. She may be a bride of Christ but to me she remains my daughter Virginia." Gone were the days of living in fear of the Vatican, Galileo now considered himself an insider. This had been his sixth audience with the Pope in four months, thanks largely to the efforts of Giovanni. Declining the offer of a carriage Galileo stepped out of the Palazzo del Quirinale into a burning June afternoon. He felt his soul required a little hardship, so he walked in the punishing heat and humidity down the hill and across the city, along the bustling Via del Plebiscito, to the Florentine church of San Giovanni Battista. Here he confessed his sins of greed and pride and knelt in prayer for forgiveness, for the lives his sins had cost, until the pain in his joints became unbearable; he limped back to his lodgings near the Pantheon and rested for the remainder of the day.

2

Ludovico delle Colombe awoke with a sense of foreboding. He was about to embark on a journey that was not without risk but would, he hoped, finally bring his feud with Galileo to an end. The intensity of the morning light assured him that his trip would at least be swift; he gave no thought to the farmers cursing the lack of rain. Ludovico had arranged passage with a salt merchant to travel from Florence to Perugia. After years of bitter rivalry and conflict between the hill-top city and the Florentine state, Ludovico had good cause to fear this journey.

    He had arranged to meet with the merchant in front of Santa Croce, but arrived early and waited in the calming shadow of the grand church. Ludovico had not been waiting long when he saw the merchant. He watched as man and beast plodded towards him with the inevitably slow, disinterested pace of mountain peasants; the merchant gazed out from the weathered narrow eyes, which, seemed to balance effortlessly between confidence and arrogance. At their first encounter Ludovico was more than a little afraid of his travelling companion-to-be, but after striking their deal he decided that it was probably as well to be in the company of a thug on this venture. They slipped out through the Porta Asinaria and set off down the Arno valley in the clear light of an autumn morning; much to Ludovico's relief the merchant's interest in commerce did not extend to conversation. And Ludovico himself was so preoccupied rehearsing his conversation with Father Caccini that he was blind to the bountiful and beautiful world around him.

They arrived at the fortified town of Arezzo sometime after None but well before Vespers; there was plenty of daylight left but the merchant would not be persuaded to press on for Perugia. Ludovico stayed at an inn near San Francesco whilst the merchant visited a relative. Ludovico was convinced that this no doubt mythical relation was probably either some other scoundrel or a whore; he would not have recognized the shadow of envy in his mind at the thought of spending an evening entwined with Mammon's daughter. Although a Florentine stronghold, Ludovico did not want to risk the unknown streets of Arezzo alone, and so he retired almost as soon as he had eaten. He told himself he was following Father Caccini's instructions to avoid being recognized but in reality he was simply afraid in a strange town.

Good to his word, the merchant collected Ludovico from the inn a little after Prime. Another bright cloudless day greeted the unlikely couple. They made good time and were approaching the Porta Sant' Angelo, around Sext, when they were stopped by a Swiss Guard. It was small relief to Ludovico that the town was under Vatican authority. The guard made a cursory search of the cart and asked their business. Feeling emboldened in the company of the merchant, Ludovico attempted a casual lie about visiting relatives. This attempt at mendacity did not suit him but the guard waved them through the gate into Perugia. The merchant brought his cart to a halt in the centre of the city and declared their journey to be at an end by asking for his payment. Ludovico now regretted that he had not made some effort to engage the merchant in conversation: he wanted to be accompanied to the very door of his appointment. In desperation Ludovico tried appealing to the merchant's sense of courtesy but failed, the contract had been fulfilled and that was all there was to it. Ludovico then spotted a potential flaw in the contractual argument, stating that their agreement was that he should be delivered to the address, but the merchant was clear about their agreement. Finally he tried pleading with the merchant and offering an additional payment, but the merchant had no interest in keeping Ludovico's company a moment longer. He was now alone in piazza Fortebraccio, his heart held fast by fear.

A tavern, just off the piazza, offered some hope of sanctuary but as he neared the gloomy entrance it seemed to mock him in the face of the joyous sun. He cautiously slipped inside. Before asking for directions, he ordered something to eat in the hope that his purchase would protect him from derision or violence. The tavern was bustling and dreary; he was convinced that every face knew the other, that a roomful of eyes was studying him as a potential source of income, an ignorant and helpless stranger. He consumed his purchase with unconscious speed and left with his information, few in the tavern noted his arrival or departure.

He had to walk almost the whole length of the ridge on to which the town was anchored before finding the tight maze of dwellings near San Domenico. He struggled, nervously, up and down the steep dark alleys, ducking under low arches certain that he had been misdirected. He convinced himself that an assailant lurked in every shadow, that he would be attacked at any moment; fear drove out from his nostrils the omnipresent scent of urine of these tight streets. Then sudden joy, sanctuary, he found the house he sought and his heart felt fit to burst; he pounded the door as if pursued by the devil himself. To his great surprise, and relief, his drum-beat was answered by Father Caccini. "My dear fellow, are you all right? Have you run all the way from Florence? Do come in."

"Thank you, thank you." Ludovico's eyes darted about the room and he collapsed into a couch by the empty fire. "Would it not have been easier for us to have met in Florence?" Ludovico gasped.

"Your letter said that you wished to discuss something of great importance and sensitivity. You can't imagine how difficult it is for me to go to Florence without either the Curia or my friends knowing. At least here there is always some official business for me to attend to." This surprised Ludovico, he had never imagined Father Caccini as someone that would have friends; rather, he considered him the sort of man for whom everyone that could be of benefit to him had a clear purpose.

Ludovico replied more calmly. "It may be difficult for you to travel anonymously but at least you have the protection of the Vatican. Whereas I have had to risk all manner of rogues and bandits."

"Yes, of course. Please accept my apologies for not giving due consideration to the difficulties a Florentine might encounter visiting this awful place. Allow me to offer you something to drink, to eat."

Ludovico gratefully accepted the offer of wine. "To refresh my mouth and drive away the foul taste of the godforsaken gruel served to me in some dreary, infested tavern. So please accept my apologies for declining your food, I have no doubt its fine flavour would be spoilt by my present condition."

"Very well, but please take your time to relax a little. Tell me, how have the past couple of years treated you? Goodness, the sun has already set in this forsaken maze." A servant was ordered to put in a fire and then dismissed for the evening.

They spent the next couple of hours exchanging summaries of their lives since they last met in Rome. Father Caccini brought the conversation around to the reason for their meeting after such a long time. "I presume our mutual acquaintance has said something of great interest for you to find it necessary for us to meet?"

"Not so much said as written. Have you read his retort to Orazio Grassi?" Ludovico did not pause to savour the fine wine he had been served.

"*The Assayer*? Of course. You haven't brought me here because of that? Don't you think I would have dragged him to sopra Minerva in chains if I had found even the slightest whiff of heresy in that rant? Oh, my friend, you had better take a care, life is too short to send men of position on the errands of fools."

Ludovico, surprising himself, replied calmly to Caccini's threat. "Buried within 'that rant' there is a subtle but deeply disturbing blasphemy, if my interpretation of the work is correct." They sat in silence, sipping wine, until Caccini's outburst evaporated. The fire was now bright. "Do you recall, in *The Assayer*, Galileo's declaration that it is motion which is the source of heat and that heat is therefore not an essential quality of a substance, as stated by Aristotle?"

"I vaguely recall something of the sort," replied Father Caccini, concentrating on the fire. Ludovico preened himself and prepared to lecture the unpredictable Dominican.

"I think we may see in this, in his thoughts on the nature of heat, a most terrible blasphemy." Ludovico paused to ensure he had Caccini's full attention. "Let me remind you of what Signor Galilei says about the qualities of substances." He produced some carefully written notes and read aloud. "*I think that tastes, odours and so on are no more than mere names so far as the object in which we place them is concerned, and that they reside only in our thoughts. Hence if the living creature were removed, all these qualities would be wiped away and annihilated.*" Ludovico paused, an invitation for Caccini to comment but none came, so he continued. "This is of course quite antithetical to the writing of Aristotle, who maintained that the qualities of substances, such as heat, cold, wet, dry, are essential to the substance itself."

"Yes? Please forgive my ignorance but this poor churchman is struggling to see where blasphemy could hide in a flavour."

Ludovico ignored Caccini's sarcasm. "Galileo claims that everything we sense, everything we feel through touch, or smell or taste are experiences only of the mind; that these qualities do not actually exist in themselves. So an apple tastes like an apple, according to Galileo, only because you experience something we call taste and have called it the taste of apple. And that there is no such quality as the taste of apple, beyond human experience, that is intrinsic to the apple."

"Very well, so there is no such thing as an apple taste unless I eat the apple and give a name to the taste. The Almighty created the world by His Word, are you suggesting that Galileo is making some sort of messianic statement on creation?" Father Caccini was more than a little perplexed but he was also intrigued and with an expansive gesture begged Ludovico to continue.

"No, not at all. Galileo goes on to propound the doctrine of atomism put forward by Democritus, who states that the smallest particles of a substance – he calls them minima – are determined only by shape and number. And it is the shape and number of these so-called minima that enter our bodies when we eat or drink, and any taste or odour is merely an accident of these minima. Furthermore, he suggests that the shape and size of each of the particles is fixed and unchanging." Ludovico paused, took some wine and gazed intently at Father Caccini, hoping to see a flicker of recognition and understanding, but he saw nothing; he was forced to continue. "You understand that what I am about to say is merely an interpretation of what Galileo has written and that I completely abhor and reject this idea?" Caccini looked puzzled by this discourse of minutia and Ludovico's could see he was waiting to hear where heresy was going to enter the discussion.

With practised grace, Father Caccini offered him reassurance.

Ludovico spoke hesitatingly. "It seems to me…" He paused, took another sip from his glass, but this minor prevarication did not make his task any easier. "It seems to me that Signor Galilei's doctrine of minima is a denial of the essential quality of substances and thus reduces taste and smell to mere elements of language."

"Yes, that much I understand. Go on," urged Caccini, his face contorted by the firelight.

"A possible conclusion one could draw from this is that the bread and wine of the Holy Sacrament of the Eucharist are mere accidents of these minima, both before and after the Sacrament. The size and shape of the minima are, according to Galileo, fixed; so no possible change can take place during the Sacrament."

Father Caccini sank into his chair, his face slipping into the darkness. He had not been prepared to hear something of this magnitude. They sat in silence for some time before he spoke.

"According to you, Galileo is claiming that all substances are made of these minima, which vary only in shape and number," Father Caccini's face re-surfaced into the firelight, "and that everything we experience through our senses is but an accident of these particles?"

"Yes."

"These minima have shape but cannot change? And from this you are suggesting that there is no transubstantiation during the Holy Sacrament of the Eucharist and that Christ cannot therefore be present during the Eucharist?"

Ludovico shrank away from Father Caccini, as if the words he had given him were contagious. He struggled to force a reply from his dry throat, his voice crackling with the fire.

"I am suggesting that Galileo's words can be interpreted in this way."

Father Caccini spoke with slow deliberation. "If you are right, Galileo would certainly go to the stake for this. If, however, you are wrong, we could both end up in Castel Sant' Angelo. We have to be extremely cautious in how we use this information." Ludovico's fear was not assuaged by Caccini's use of "we". "Have you discussed this interpretation with anyone else?"

"Absolutely not."

"Good. I presume you are aware of the friendship that exists between Galileo and His Holiness? When last in Rome he was parading around like a peacock, he is more insufferable than ever now that he has a friend seated in the Vatican. Let us discuss this further in the morning." Father Caccini led Ludovico to a modest bedchamber. The evening's conversation had opened the gates for all manner of demons and doubts to flood and charge around Ludovico's mind; neither wish nor prayer could bring sleep to his dervish thoughts. He longed for the morning with a greater hunger than he had ever known.

Sunlight and the world were eventually reunited. Father Caccini insisted that Ludovico accompany him to the Prime service at San Domenico. The virgin light of morning had not yet penetrated the near subterranean alleys as they groped their way up to San Domenico, and the streets lurked in an unnatural darkness that was pierced with occasional bursts of brightness.

Father Caccini spoke purposefully. "I spent the remainder of last evening in prayer seeking guidance. It could be extremely dangerous for us to openly accuse Signor Galilei of such a heinous heresy."

Ludovico could not believe his ears; the man who had originally denounced Galileo now spoke of caution. But Ludovico was resigned to his fate, he had voluntarily released his words and was now a prisoner of Caccini's will. He could not imagine that Father Caccini would do anything to put himself at risk, so the closer he stayed to Caccini the safer he should be.

"I shall send you information regarding the thirteenth session of the Council of Trent, which ruled on the Holy Sacrament of the Eucharist. I then want you to put your observations on *The Assayer* in a letter, within the context of the ruling of the Council."

Ludovico stopped dead and grabbed Father Caccini. "You want me to put this in writing? Are you mad? Do you want me sent to the stake?" Ludovico was screaming, the distorted sound of his voice bouncing off the walls, as he pinned Caccini against the rotten brickwork and almost smashed his head on a low arch.

"Signor delle Colombe," Father Caccini demanded imperiously, "please release me and stop acting like a frightened child." Ludovico released Father Caccini absentmindedly, as if he was somehow unaware of his own actions. "When, all those years ago," Caccini continued, "I first denounced Galileo from the pulpit of Santa Maria Novella, I acted with certainty. I stood squarely in the pulpit, my feet growing out of its stonework, so that I and the pulpit and the pillar were a harmonious whole, I felt as if I were a part of the very fabric of Santa Maria. And when the congregation turned towards me, I saw the power of that certainty in their faces, their eyes wide and their ears open. Nothing has happened since that day to weaken my faith in this cause." Ludovico's concerns were crushed by the power of Caccini's delivery. "So you see, we are fixed on a course that cannot fail or harm us because in faith it is right." Caccini gave himself a moment to savour his own words. "I do not want you to sign this letter, I simply need a legitimate reason to bring this theory of yours to the attention of His Holiness. So, you will produce an anonymous letter, which you will then send to the Chief Inquisitor, Father Giustino, in the Commissary General's Office. He is a good man and may be trusted. The letter will then come into my possession and I will take it personally to His Holiness. The friendship between Galileo and Pope Urban is common knowledge and it would therefore be quite reasonable for me to take such a delicate and important matter to him directly. Indeed, I should expect that His Holiness will want to demonstrate his gratitude towards the man that has given his personal position such judicious consideration. But to the task in hand: Galileo's book does not mention the Holy Sacrament of the Eucharist, and the general point you have noted is obtuse to say the least, thus others in the Curia may have a different interpretation. Nevertheless, I am sure His Holiness will smell the faggots of heresy when I bring this to his attention, but it will be far too embarrassing for him and Holy Mother Church to pursue unless forced to do so. An accord of some sort will be reached."

"Given that this is such a dangerous route for us to take with little, if any, secure outcome, why should we take the risk at all?" Although a seasoned courtier, Ludovico was, rightly, afraid at getting too close to the machinations of Vatican politics. Father Caccini presented himself as a master of the art of political manipulation but this was of no great comfort to Ludovico.

"The very least we can expect from this foray," Caccini proclaimed, "will be to strain, perhaps even break, the bonds of friendship between pontiff and mathematician; with that bond broken, who can say what other opportunities may present themselves to the detriment of Signor Galilei?"

3

Galileo's housekeeper, Maria, snapped awake to the sound of beating on the door. She had been dozing in the cool of the kitchen, and so it took a moment or two for her to orientate herself. Moving reluctantly from slumber she opened the heavy oak door and was immediately bathed in bright light and warm air. Her eyes adjusted slowly to the sudden brightness to reveal Galileo's son standing on the lowest of three steps, at eye level with Maria. He looked at her with his father's eyes but they lacked his penetrating intensity.

"Signor Vincenzio, what an uncommon surprise."

"Hello, Maria. So this is the new casa Galilei? It's certainly a long enough walk from the city. But I must say it looks splendid."

"Your father doesn't complain about the walk. Indeed, he considers this house something of a jewel." Maria had long since given up attempting to conceal the contempt she felt for a man she considered a spoilt wastrel.

"Of course. Has he returned from Rome?" Asked Vincenzio dismissively.

"He got home yesterday; he's up on the loggia resting. I suppose you want to disturb him?"

"A loggia! Finally we are moving up in the world. That will be useful for his observations, I am sure."

"Have you taken up an interest in astronomy since you last graced us with your presence?" Vincenzio did not respond.

Maria escorted Vincenzio via the kitchen so that she could collect a jug of lemon squash with which to awaken Galileo, who was still recovering from his week-long journey from Rome to Florence. The air was thick with the scent of summer laziness. Maria shook him gently and whispered, "Maestro, signor, signor. Here, I have brought you a fresh drink."

Galileo stirred from a deep sleep, mumbling his words of thanks. After the first slight sip, he drank deeply.

"Signor Vincenzio is here to see you," Maria said.

"Oh. Thank you, show him up." The glass now empty, Galileo's mouth still searched for the invigorating liquid. "And could you bring up something more to drink please."

Maria waved Vincenzio out onto the loggia from the doorway, where she had instructed him to wait, and returned to the kitchen.

"Father... Your eye...?" Galileo's left eye was red-raw and misty.

"It's nothing, it will pass in a day or two."

Vincenzio accepted his father's word without further thought or enquiry. "Most noble and beloved father, I come to congratulate you on your visit to Rome and commend you on this fine new home."

"Yes, of course. Please give me a moment, Cenzo, sit down." Galileo sat up on the couch and shuffled about distractedly whilst preparing himself for another request for money that he could not afford to give. He still had the headache that had sent him to the couch and was grateful when Maria returned with another carafe of squash.

Galileo had the loggia built with a southerly aspect and his neighbours thought he was mad to do this when any sane person would want to avoid the summer sun, but he had increasing need of Phoebus' soothing balm. And he had designed the end of the loggia as an open terrace with a raised platform for his observations. "So, Cenzo, what do you think of *ill Gioiello*?"

"It looks to be a beautiful house, Father, and with such a wonderful position its attraction for you is clear. That must be San Matteo?" Vincenzio pointed at a grey collection of buildings beyond the orchard as he spoke but he did not wait for his father would wax lyrical on his favourite child. "Though it is a little far from the hum of the city for my tastes."

"Yes, you would need to exercise your legs to find a tavern."

Ignoring this sarcasm Vincenzio continued, "I had rather hoped, beloved Father, to hear of your trip to the Holy City."

Pleasantly surprised by Vincenzio's apparent interest, Galileo spared no detail of his numerous audiences with Pope Urban or of his meeting and feasting with noble Romans. He spoke with great animation and vigour during this expansive description of his Roman sojourn. "For the first time since the death of Duke Cosimo, I feel the warm security of being an insider again. These past years have carried all the torment and tedium of the wilderness but that is all to change now." Almost as an aside, he added, "And you will be pleased to hear that I have managed to acquire a small pension for you."

"Oh Father, that is wonderful news! I finally become a member of court."

"No, I am afraid not, Cenzo. The pension is a gift from His Holiness in honour of my work. You will be expected to carry out some minor ecclesiastical duties, nothing too taxing for you. You have been offered a position as canon to the parish of Brescia with an income of sixty scudi a year. This is not a great deal but it will go some way to meeting your endless debts. It will certainly save me money."

"What? I am expected to shave my head in that ridiculous fashion and be sent to some forsaken village. Father, if you want me dead just kill me, but I will not accept this banishment."

"Cenzo, please don't exaggerate in that foolish way of yours. This is a non-residential canonry – do you really believe I would plan to send you away? You will be expected to carry out the most minor of occasional duties and, yes, you will have to wear a tonsure. A small price to pay for a regular income that does not demand any real work."

"I had hoped for a place at court, as the legitimate son of the eminent philosopher to the Medici Court. It is my right to be recognized at court, where else am I to find a suitable wife?"

"Oh, surely; you know full well that Duke Cosimo legitimated you so there is no question of your being deemed socially acceptable to the court. But since the Duke's death I am in no position to plead for a court sinecure on your behalf, the Duchess Christina does not have the interests of the late Duke. Think of this canonry as an opportunity for you to develop your position in society."

"Father, I cannot accept this meagre pension, it is beneath my rank and status."

Exasperated by his son, Galileo spat out: "What is that you say?"

"Such a pension may suit some filthy monk, but I should have a place at court with an appropriate pension." Vincenzio's face red glowed with anger.

"If it is not beneath you to turn your head, cast your eyes over there to the bell tower of San Matteo." Galileo's calm demeanour belied the depth of his anger and disappointment, but he made no effort to conceal his contempt for his own blood. "For over four hundred years, there has been a monastery there. Four hundred years of prayers for the salvation of others, holy men living simple lives of faith, spending long hours in prayer, praying with hands filthy and callused from toil. And you consider the support of Holy Mother Church beneath you. Your sisters live there in desperate poverty; they too live in prayer for us: you, me, everyone. They do not consider the vanities of earthly wealth; their hearts and souls are set on eternal salvation. I am dumbstruck at how you could consider a pension offered personally by His Holiness himself to be beneath you." Galileo paused to regain his breath, and now spoke with acerbic softness. "Cenzo, I have no doubt that you have already earned yourself a place in the fourth circle of Hell, but try not to sink any lower. May the Lord strike me, but I do not know how I could have brought such a craven individual into this world. You had better leave this house before the thighs you pay for warmth go cold." Galileo closed his eyes and collapsed back into the couch. The excitement that had given him such vitality had now been usurped by disappointed resignation drawn taut across his face.

Vincenzio tried to speak but his mouth remained resolutely closed. He left the house quietly.

Galileo sat motionless listening intently to the unquestioning activity of the birds and cicada; regaining his composure, he went down to the kitchen and cleared his head with some cold water. "Maria, would you make up a sack of fruit, please? I am going over to San Matteo."

"Don't you think you should rest a little more? At least let me come with you to carry the sack." Vincenzio's visits always upset Galileo and Maria often had to provide soothing words to her master when his son had left.

"No, thank you, the walk will do me good and the mule can carry the fruit."

He led the mule across the shallow valley through the orchard, accompanied by the sound of dry grass crunching underfoot. He entered the silent courtyard of San Matteo and, after tying the mule to the gate, sat on a bench built into the wall. The grey stone of the courtyard felt cool and serene as Galileo waited for the Poor Clares to finish the None service his eyes slowly closed.

"Papa, Papa, can we play the ball game again?" asked the little girl in her singsong voice as she bound into Galileo's study, a large untidy room that Marina, the mother of his children, refused to enter as she considered it to be more like a carpenter's workshop than the study of a university professor.

"Of course, sweetheart, just give Papa a moment to sort out his papers." He cleared some space on a large desk and lifted a narrow ramp of about two metres in length and a metre tall at its high end with a small bell at the bottom. He then picked up the nine-year-old Virginia to stand on a stool, they had played this game a lot in the past months and he revelled in her enjoyment and interest in his experiments. He placed a ball at the top of the ramp and Virginia held it in place by lightly placing a finger on it.

"Ready?" asked Galileo, and when he nodded his head, she released the ball. Using his pulse, he timed the ball's descent until the bell rang. They played this game with balls of all sizes, weights and materials until Virginia's mother, Marina, summoned them for supper. Galileo was thrilled and inspired by the interest and enjoyment displayed by his young assistant.

Galileo awoke to a rough hand gently stroking his arm.

"Oh Virginia, I was just thinking about you."

"Dearest Papa, what a lovely surprise."

It took a few moments for Galileo to wake up and focus properly. His eyes felt sticky and a little bleary.

"What have you done to your eye?" asked Virginia. Galileo ignored the question, his eyes scanning the faces flowing past from the service.

"Child, you look pale and wan, are you ill? Where is Livia?" But Virginia was not so easily put off.

"Papa, have you seen the apothecary for a poultice or ointment?"

"Daughter, you know full well that I know more than most that aspire to medicine. So where is your sister, why is Livia not with you?"

"Sister Archangela, Father, remains in her bed. She has a mild fever but will, I am sure, soon be well. As for myself, I am well and feel strong despite appearances." They sat together on the stone bench that grew out of the convent wall.

"Now tell me all about Rome, you saw His Holiness?"

"His Holiness favoured me with many audiences." Galileo related his visit with no detail too small for Virginia's hungry curiosity. "In addition to this bag of fruit, I also bring news from His Holiness. He has agreed to arrange for a Visitator for San Matteo, indeed the Pope's private secretary gave me his personal assurance that he will make the necessary arrangements."

"Oh Papa, the Mother Abbess will be so pleased to hear that. We have had such a terrible time with unreliable visiting Fathers taking advantage of our poor community."

"Well, that is all to end now, as you will be getting a hand-picked Franciscan Father. However, I have saved my best news till last. His Holiness has given his support to my resuming my work and that I may make use of the Copernican hypothesis. So I can now return to my work on tides." Virginia's face fell at this news. "What is the matter, child? I thought you of all people would be pleased."

"I fear for you, Papa." Her voice dropped to little more than a whisper. "You still have enemies in the Collegio Romano and the Curia, and I doubt that His Holiness can protect you against them all. And if you use your astronomical observations to prove that the cause of the tides is the movement of the earth about the sun you will be moving from hypothesis to physical truth. There are many that would not hesitate to denounce you as a heretic for that, even though I and His Holiness know that to be far from the truth. Papa, I implore you to seek some other avenue for your great mind. Surely this world has so much to offer your eyes and clear sight that this dangerous business could be left to some other?" Virginia's keen mind was always able to follow Galileo's thinking, far better indeed than most of his students; although proud of her devotion to the Church, it always saddened him that society prevented her from being able to follow a university career.

"Ha! Who sees the world as I do? Have no fear, child, Maffeo will look after me. Now tell me, have you been able to repair my shirts?"

Virginia, recognizing that this topic of discussion was now closed, took up her father's domestic enquiry. "Yes, I have made new collars and cuffs. Actually if you would be kind enough to provide me with a good piece of linen I will make a new shirt for Cenzo. I hear his clothes are looking rather threadbare these days. Have you seen him since your return?"

"I will not waste any breath discussing that fool disgrace of my name."

"Papa, do try to be more patient with Cenzo. We may all have your name but we cannot have your mind as well. Cenzo is but a weak child, the Lord teaches us that the weak need our love and charity, not chiding."

Humbled by the wisdom of his daughter, he said no more about his son. Galileo left his Virginia with that special pain of parting from a loved one.

4

With obsequious civility, Father Caccini kissed the silken slippers of His Holiness Pope Urban VIII. He knelt, waiting for his instruction to rise.

"Father Caccini, it is something of a surprise for us to be pressed so ardently to give an audience to a member of the Dominican Order without knowing the full details of the pretext for such an honour."

"I am grateful to Your Holiness for allowing this humble servant of Holy Mother Church an opportunity of discourse with you. I can assure you that this is a matter of the utmost delicacy and sensitivity which requires your personal attention. Were this not the case, I would not have prevailed so to speak directly to your Holiness and I beg your forgiveness for my intrusion."

"Yes, we are sure that you have the good works of Holy Mother Church always at heart." Caccini remained impassive at the Pope's obvious sarcasm. "Now please do not keep us in suspense a moment longer."

Father Caccini shuffled slightly and looked over to the Pope's private secretary. "I must repeat, Your Holiness, that this is a matter of extreme delicacy." His eyes darted back and forth between Giovanni and Pope Urban as he spoke.

"Are you suggesting that this matter is of so delicate a nature that not even our private secretary should be privy to it?"

Caccini fought to stay calm, it had taken him months of lobbying to get this audience and if he failed to deliver his news now he would not get another opportunity to speak directly with the pontiff.

"I am merely suggesting, Holiness, that you may wish to consider the highly sensitive matter in hand before deciding with whom to share the information." Caccini placed sufficient emphasis on the "you" for Urban to recognize that this affected him directly. Pope Urban sat silent for some moments stroking his short square beard, the scratching of Giovanni's busy pen echoing around the room.

"Giovanni, please give Father Caccini a few moments with us." The private secretary silently left the audience chamber. This apparently casual request was in reality a clear instruction for Giovanni to retire no farther than the other side of the closed door and to return within five minutes.

"Thank you, Your Holiness. I shall come straight to the point. A letter has recently come into my possession that purports to make observations on the recent work by Signor Galilei. These observations, if found to be true, and I sincerely hope that this is not the case, do, I fear, point to a most heinous heresy. Being cognizant of your acquaintance with Signor Galilei, and thus the potential embarrassment posed to Your Beatitude, I felt that I should bring the missive personally and immediately to your attention." Caccini slowly drew the letter from his habit and took a slight step back as he handed it to the Pontiff. Urban read the letter three or four times before speaking.

"An anonymous letter, it seems our epistle writer does not have the courage of his convictions."

"Indeed not, Your Holiness." Father Caccini decided that having got the letter before the Pope the best course of action was to say as little as possible and leave as soon as possible. He gambled that, although His Holiness might suspect him of being the author of the letter, he stood on fairly safe ground as the Pope would not want to initiate an unnecessary and potentially damaging inquiry. But he had to remain calm, to respond to questions with clear deliberation, carefully concealing any lies under a veil of truth.

"Opinions expressed in anonymity are surely to be viewed with caution, as some hidden motive will lie behind the author's desire to remain unknown. Which rather brings his opinions into question. Was the letter addressed to you personally?" asked Urban, holding Caccini in his gaze.

"No, Your Holiness; it came to my attention via the Commissary General's Office." Father Caccini glanced downwards as he spoke.

"I see. To whom in the Commissary General's Office was it sent?"

"I am afraid I do not know, Your Holiness."

"Perhaps then you have some insight as to why the Commissary General's Office saw fit to seek your opinion on such a dangerous and scandalous letter?"

Although Father Caccini's had expected this line of questioning about his official role, his mouth was dry. He was about to reply when Giovanni slipped back into the audience chamber; Pope Urban, with the slightest of hand gestures, sent him back out.

"I believe it was my knowledge of Tridentine law that was sought."

"We were not aware of your expertise in this area. So, the Commissary General saw fit to send the letter to you rather than directly to the Curia for a legal opinion?"

It was time to be bold, Caccini risked all on not being directly challenged on a lie.

"It is as you see, Your Holiness. I cannot comment on the daily operations of the Commissary General's Office, I cannot even say whether or not the Commissary General is personally aware of the letter."

Urban's gaze returned to the letter, Caccini felt sure he was debating with himself on whether or not to press him on the provenance of the letter. "Very well, let us return to your professed area of expertise. Pray provide us with your legal opinion."

Now on relatively safe ground, Father Caaini spoke with unhesitating confidence. "It is certainly the case that Canon Two, of the thirteenth session of the Sacred Council of Trent of 1541 states that should anyone deny the Transubstantiation of the Blessed Holy Sacrament he should be declared anathema. Indeed this is stated, in varying forms, in all eleven Canons of the thirteenth session."

"Are you suggesting that the letter could have been written by a churchman?"

Father Caccini was suddenly conscious of his palms sweating profusely. "That is, of course, possible, Your Holiness. However, although the legal position stated by this letter is accurate I cannot comment on the observations made by Signor Galilei of the physical properties of these tiny particles. Clearly, if this interpretation of Signor Galilei's book were found to be true..." Caccini allowed his voice to trail off and spoke in incomplete, barely coherent phrases. "I cannot even begin to imagine the difficulties... the punishment... such a diabolic heresy."

"Indeed. At least you can be grateful then that you are not a theological advisor to the Congregation of the Index," snapped Pope Urban. Father Caccini offered profuse apologies for his impertinence. With brusque swiftness Pope Urban thanked Father Caccini for bringing the letter to his attention. "Your consideration for the well being of Holy Mother Church in this matter is, of course, noted. We shall have this examined by someone qualified to comment reliably on the physical observations before we make any judgement. As you are aware of the great sensitivity of this matter, I know that you will not discuss its contents with anyone beyond this room. You may be assured that we will seek due and proper consultation on this matter." Father Caccini acknowledged the thinly veiled warning and took his leave of the Pope.

It was some moments after Caccini's departure that Giovanni returned to the audience chamber. Pope Urban was incandescent with rage, Giovanni gently pulled the door shut behind him and waited until spoken to.

"Giovanni, there will be no further audiences today."

"But, Your Holiness…" Urban raised the palm of his hand to Giovanni.

"I don't care who or what is listed for today, just go…" Urban was shocked by the sudden realization that he was barking at Giovanni; he continued more calmly, "Please send out messages to whomsoever and join us in our chapel."

"Yes, Your Holiness."

Urban's private chapel was a small cell-like room, dimly lit with only a small window high in the wall and a few candles. The room was filled with the odour of paint and plaster, no amount of incense could disguise the smell; the walls covered with frescoes recording the Passion of Christ had only recently been completed. The candlelight flickering on the vivid colours brought the images to life. Urban knelt before a huge painting of the deposition. Despite the clearly devotional function of the room, Urban could not resist having his pontifical cartouche placed in each corner at the ceiling. Some two or three hours had passed before Giovanni joined Urban in his private chapel, the pontiff was exhausted and spoke wearily. "Ah, Giovanni, please come."

"Thank you, Holiness."

"I am afraid that Leo has put us in an impossibly embarrassing and difficult predicament."

"Leo? Signor Galilei, Your Holiness?" Giovanni was not aware of any recent correspondence with Galileo.

"Yes, Leo. What do you think of this letter?" Giovanni re-read the letter several times before he spoke.

"Your Holiness, I think this letter is a monstrous slur against a great and faithful philosopher."

"So do I. I am certain that this scurrilous missive is theologically unsound, to say the least. Father Caccini is a mischievous and scheming man and I would not be surprised to learn that he had something to do with this vile note. Although to a learned churchman this apparent denial of Transubstantiation is, I am certain, fundamentally wrong, to a simple layman, or those with a grudge to bear, it could appear to be an *a priori* blasphemy. We cannot afford to give Father Caccini any opportunity to bring this to his vindictive pulpit. I will not have the reputation of this papacy and the offices of Holy Mother Church brought into question by anyone, even if that means cutting off an old friend. I am afraid that today we have lost the brightest of stars from our court. However, we are at least fortunate that Leo is not in Rome." Urban's voice tailed off.

Giovanni spoke on behalf of their friend. "I am sure Signor Galilei in all of his brilliant works acts with only good will towards Your Holiness and Holy Mother Church."

"That is of no consequence now. I thank the Lord that when he was last in Rome I was not tempted to revoke the position authorised by his Beatitude Pope Paul the Fifth on the Copernican hypothesis." Pointing towards the letter in Giovanni's hand Urban continued: "Henceforth we will not have any direct communications with Signor Galilei whatsoever, I know I can rely on your loyalty in this matter."

"Holiness, er… Signor Galilei is perhaps the finest natural philosopher in the…"

"I hope I can rely on your loyalty?" demanded Urban.

Giovanni responded without further hesitation. "Your Holiness may be assured of my loyalty; I recognize that a situation such as this puts all personal considerations aside for the greater good of Holy Mother Church. You need never doubt my sincerity on this, Your Holiness."

Satisfied with this response, Urban now spoke with his soft mellifluous voice. "Thank you, Giovanni. We shall both suffer the pain of putting aside a friendship; your loyalty to Holy Mother Church will receive its due reward in the Glory of Heaven. Kneel here with me, let us pray and give thanks for the rewards we have been granted by the Lord." They knelt in silent prayer for almost an hour before Urban rose and sat on his couch, refreshed and calm.

"Giovanni, arrange for a consultant to examine and dismiss this letter. But ensure that our consultant is a Dominican, so that if his decision should, at some later date, be found to be in error we cannot be seen to have been remiss in our duty. I would like you to carry out this task personally, quickly and with due decorum. We cannot risk any unnecessary tongue-wagging. I am particularly concerned that we do not give that dog Caccini the slightest opportunity to raise this ugly matter with us again."

"I understand, Your Holiness." Giovanni was quick to respond but the Pope gave no suggestion as to how his high-profile private secretary might carry out a surreptitious investigation.

Pope Urban added, "Indeed, I think we should also arrange to take a closer interest in the pulpit pronouncements of Father Caccini and I am sure it would do no harm for Caccini to be aware of our interest in his sermons."

"Yes, Holiness."

"Finally, and this will be most difficult for us, should Signor Galilei fall foul of the Congregations of the Index or the Inquisition at any time in the future, we shall be compelled to pursue him with the full weight of the law, and give him no quarter." He gave no indication to Giovanni that they warn Galileo of his now tenuous relationship with the Holy Office. Pope Urban had stated there should be absolutely no direct contact with Galileo and that is precisely what he meant.

5

Giovanni spent the winter and most of the spring making the surreptitious enquiries directed by His Holiness. This slow tangential work eventually led him to the name of a Dominican who had previously had dealings with Galileo. As fortune would have it, the man was in Rome attending to the sick on Tiber Island. Although the man he sought lived under the very nose of the Vatican, it left Giovanni with something of a problem in that only mill workers and the sick went to Tiber Island. He had no business with millers and the sick were best avoided. He pondered long on how to get to the island without meeting some acquaintance that might draw attention to his visit. All routes carried the risk of discovery; he chose the route by which he was least likely to be recognized but which also placed him at greatest danger of physical harm.

Giovanni headed south from the western end of the Vatican complex, then re-entered the city enclosure at porte Aurelio and travelled through the Jewish ghetto towards the river. As a gentile in this part of Rome, he attracted quite some attention but at least no one knew his identity; it was with more than a little relief that he crossed to Tiber Island via ponte Cestio, the bridge led directly to the church of San Bartolomeo and the Fatebenefratelli hospital.

Light streamed through the windows of the main hall of the hospital, ethereal buttresses supporting the walls; the matte of the dry floor contrasted sharply with the glassy shine of the freshly cleaned wet floor, which a friar was scrubbing with the focus and determination of an ancient ascetic. Giovanni's shoes made a soft phlat, phlat sound as he cautiously stepped over the boundary of the dry to the wet, hoping not to wake any patients nor leave marks on the scrubbed flagstones. He spoke in an urgent whisper. "Excuse me, Father, I am seeking Father Baccarini."

"Yes?" replied the friar without pause in his rhythmic scrubbing.

"Father, I humbly beseech you, I must speak with Father Baccarini on a matter of great import."

"All God's work is a matter of 'great import'." He continued scrubbing. Giovanni knelt and spoke directly into his ear, beginning to lose his patience.

"I have been sent by the Bishop of Rome to gather an opinion from Father Baccarini." Silence, the scrubbing stopped.

"Opinions are cheap and easily gathered, the Curia spends its time manufacturing them; perhaps His Holiness should seek one there."

"His Holiness does not send his personal secretary on such errands lightly." Giovanni lost his battle to keep his growing irritation from his voice, and glanced around the room to see if he had awoken any of the infirm: if any were awake they were not in any condition to listen with care. The friar looked up and Giovanni stared back with honest eyes. Although Giovanni did not wear the insignia of the Holy See, the friar's experience and instincts must have told him that he spoke the truth.

"I will join you in the garden vestibule when I have finished. Take the stairs to the right of the door you entered by and follow them to the bottom."

Giovanni withdrew, his cautious walk now silent on the dry floor. He waited for almost an hour before the Father joined him; the occasional passing friar neither acknowledged nor spoke to him. This did not ease his anxiety. Giovanni introduced himself formally and produced a seal of the Holy See to confirm his identity. "You are Father Cesare Baccarini, formerly of the Congregation of the Inquisition?"

"Yes."

"Father, the matter I wish to discuss with you is of such sensitivity that I would prefer that no one ever know my true identity or the reason for my visit."

"That should not be difficult, as I have no idea what it is you require of me."

"Can we talk somewhere where we can be certain there are no additional ears?"

"Let us walk in the kitchen garden, there will be few brothers working whilst the sun pours out its heat to the full." They walked from the cool shade of the vestibule into the blinding brilliance and heat of a late spring sun. They stopped at the end of the garden, the end of the island overlooked by the single remaining arch of a Roman bridge, a lone sentinel from a bygone age of greatness now a useless ruin in the middle of the river.

"Father, His Holiness has asked that I gather an opinion on a certain letter and I believe that you are ideally placed to offer a view."

"Ah, do you hear that? Do you hear the bees busy about their business?"

Giovanni ignored this oft-repeated jibe at the three bees on the Barberini coat of arms that, as Pope Urban, Maffeo transferred to his papal cartouche. "Please accept my apologies for this intrusion, Father, but this matter is a source of great vexation to His Holiness; had it not been necessary to break into your quietude I can assure I would not have done so."

"No, of course not." Father Baccarini showed little interest in matters that personally concerned His Holiness.

Giovanni continued, ignoring Baccarini's dismissive grunts and removed a letter from his tunic.

"I must stress once more, Father, that this is a matter of the utmost sensitivity and that you must never disclose the contents of this letter or our discussion."

"Signor Ciàmpoli, although I am no longer a member of the Congregation of the Inquisition, and have not been so for quite some years now, I remain bound by that vow of secrecy."

"Of course. My humble apologies, Father, I know you to be a man of exemplary repute and have no wish to offend you. This letter has come into the possession of His Holiness and he wishes to gather an independent opinion about its content before deciding what action, if any, to take. When you read it I think you will understand why His Holiness did not wish to go directly to the Curia for a view." Giovanni handed over the missive that Father Caccini had given to Pope Urban. Father Baccarini read intently and sank into the short wall on which they sat, his gaze lost on some distant point.

"Signor Galilei... investigation 1181... my last..." Father Baccarini addressed some unseen confident. "As chief inquisitor I examined the lives of many souls in order to determine whether or not they had acted or thought in a manner contrary to the teachings and direction of Holy Mother Church. Witnesses were sought and questioned, depositions written on their behalf and signed; other pertinent documents examined. A process was followed and if the process were adhered to diligently the correct outcome could be assured. At least that was what I believed until the case of Signor Galilei."

"What happened?" Giovanni gently asked.

"As I have already pointed out, I remain subject to my vow of secrecy. However, I am sure you will have already deduced that the usual protocols did not appear to have been followed."

"I see." Giovanni was desperate to know what had actually happened but he respected the Father's integrity and did not want to risk offending him; it was clear that Father Baccarini was not a man one could quiz with circumlocutions.

"It was not until that investigation, in about sixteen fifteen or sixteen, that I realized the administrative process of that great pillar of the Congregation of the Inquisition could be manipulated. Its apparent strength is also its weakness, which is to say that power and primacy is given to the testimony of paper over the speech of individuals: paper is their Achilles heel. I had given little serious thought to the possibility of falsified documents, you know the sort of thing: orders, charters, wills, depositions and the like, after all most are written by Holy Mother Church. This may sound naïve to you but I had an unflinching faith in the administration of the Congregation of the Inquisition; the good works we carried out on behalf of Holy Mother Church to save her souls. Once my faith in the process had been shaken, I began to question the outcomes of all the cases I had investigated. It near drove me mad: cases, questions, my faith, all whirring about my head in a storm. Until, that is, I accepted that in my role as a searcher of truth of heart I had almost certainly reached some ill-considered conclusions and had consequently done harm to my fellow, innocent, man. Now, here, I insist on carrying out the most menial and unpleasant of tasks in an effort, albeit in some small way, to atone for the sins I have committed." Father Baccarini let the letter drop to the ground, and clasped his hands in prayer.

"Signor Galilei, was that case an error?" Giovanni, keen to know more about his friend's case, gently seized his opportunity.

"We may never know. Once the administrative procedure has been compromised it is almost impossible to know where truth and falsehood lie; all I know for certain is that the case did not follow the usual procedure. Draw from that what you will. I certainly no longer have faith in the administration of the Congregation and once that is gone one cannot have confidence in its findings… And paper, oh paper, this may yet prove itself to be the most pernicious and evil of man's inventions… the evil that may be spun on paper. These days it is printed with mechanical words and sent around the world. The greatness of the evil of paper is that when it is made to lie no one will accept a truth that is contrary to that set down unless there is more paper to act as proof. The Word of God, the breath from His lips, created the universe; Moses's commandments were written in stone by the finger of God; the hand of the Almighty wrote on the wall of Nebuchadnezzar's hall. Truly, the hands of men put the Word into the Holy Bible, men of God, holy men whose hands were guided by the Lord. These days, men from any walk of life may put pen or print to paper, men who are not of God, men who may even commit evil deeds through writing. Documents need no longer be written by hand, books can be produced in great number, and to say what? What need is there for more than the Word of God? Holy Mother Church is right to attempt to control the production of books, but for how long will She have that power? Those that wish to wield great power will do so by controlling printed pages. If you doubt me, consider the strife created by Luther spreading his vile accusations against Holy Mother Church. No, my friend, kill a man with a knife and there will be somewhere a witness that can put man, knife and victim together; kill a man with paper and no one will ever know a crime has been done." Father Baccarini fell silent again. After what felt like a seemly period Giovanni spoke in hushed tones.

"Father, following your discourse on documents and truth, what is your opinion of the letter?" Giovanni had to ask several times before Father Baccarini responded.

"I am sorry, please excuse the ravings of an old fool."

"No, Father, I see that you have paid a great price for your faith. I can only pray to be able to follow your purity of faith, staunch integrity and steadfast example." Giovanni spoke from his heart.

"This letter is a fine example of the mischief that can be spread by the written word. Your letter writer is an ignorant, ill-read churchman; however, he is also dangerous because he understands the power of well-placed words. This letter is clearly intended to damn Signor Galilei but no well-read churchman could take it seriously. Indeed, I am sure His Holiness has read the most venerable Saint Aquinas closely enough to see through this tissue of errant lies."

"Pray indulge me, Father."

"In the *Summa Theologiæ*, Saint Thomas Aquinas discusses transubstantiation with great erudition. To be brief, he concludes that the presence of Christ's true body and blood, during the Blessed Holy Sacrament of the Eucharist, cannot be detected by sense or understanding but by faith alone. So, all of the trouble your letter writer goes to with regard to minima and essences and sensations is wasted, for he has misunderstood the fundamental meaning of the most Blessed Holy Sacrament of the Eucharist and Transubstantiation: Our Lord Jesus Christ is Sacramentally present as an act of faith."

"So there is no heresy in this letter?"

"None whatsoever, though it saddens me greatly that Saint Thomas is not being as closely read in Rome as he should be."

"Father, I thank you for your time and wisdom. Now, please, is there anything at all I can do for you; I am not without influence."

"I am sure you speak the truth, but we are all condemned to live in the shadow of our past and make our amends to our Lord Almighty who will weigh our wrongs."

III

1
1631

It was a misty summer morning as émigrés from the Tuscan state gathered at the church of Saint John the Baptist de' Fiorentini. The martyrdom of St John the Baptist is an important day in the calendar for Florentines living in Rome, at least for those that have endured the summer in the city or returned early from their villas. Although not yet complete, their new church is dedicated to the protector of Florence, St John the Baptist, and provides hospital care and alms for the Florentines of Rome. Construction of the church had been funded by members of the Compagnia della Pietà, who had for years provided help and succour to the poor and infirm Florentines of Rome. The feast day was the occasion on which to be seen providing for those less fortunate than oneself: for anyone with intentions or pretensions to goodness to be seen by those of power and influence and to make new business contacts.

Federico had a prior embassy engagement and so Caterina, as wife of the ambassador, represented the pinnacle of Florentine society in Rome. After the service she held a small court, moving along the aisle. In the side chapels, merchants and contractors were bartering their deals, buying goods, selling wares and agreeing contracts for services, all in sight of Saint Jerome pursuing his writing.

As Caterina reached the foot of the church steps she stopped and turned, her ladies-in-waiting and other courtiers were surprised and confused by this unplanned moment and tried to hurry her along to her carriage but she resisted. The huge figure of Father Riccardi began to descend the church steps, slowly, hesitantly; he saw Caterina looking expectantly towards him.

"Caterina my child," he called out with a warm smile. "What a pleasure it is, as always, to see you, but I hope that this does not mean that our ambassador is unwell?"

"No, not at all. He is, I am afraid, the prisoner of embassy business." She spoke gaily, motioning that Riccardi should join her. "Leave us!" she snapped at her entourage, and took a few paces into Piazza Dell Oro with Father Riccardi. "Now, Uncle, what is this I hear about Leo's book being delayed by your office? I am surprised at you, I must say." In an effort to make light of her enquiry, she spoke with the teasing sing-song voice of a little girl.

Riccardi momentarily appeared taken aback by this sudden questioning of Vatican business. "Ah, my sweet child. I wish that matters were so simple, but between the theological debates and the positioning of the Holy See, this is a most complex matter." Caterina shot him a harsh glance, cutting short his condescension. "Very well, I am sorry but... Listen, between you and me," he bent his ungainly frame to speak softly in her ear, "His Holiness himself has taken quite an interest in this book and it has not helped matters." He straightened up, his face bearing a look that fell somewhere between wounded pride and self-pity.

"I see the difficulty for you, but you are Master of the Sacred Palace, a role of quite some import and influence; this is a matter of Tuscan pride, which the duke is very keen to see concluded to his satisfaction." The impassivity in Caterina's tone gave a hard edge to her presence.

Father Riccardi smiled softly as he spoke. "Yes, I know, I feel the matter most keenly, I can assure you. I wonder, do you think it might be possible to approach Prince Cesi to make representation to the Curia to try to unblock the situation?"

"Alas, the noble Prince Cesi is at his estate in Aquasparta and I have heard that he is quite unwell. So I am afraid you will have to see what you can do. I know that you have the skill, wisdom and position to resolve this situation." Caterina now injected her voice with bright optimism, and grabbing his arm she reached up and placed a kiss on Riccardi's cheek. "It is always a joy to see you, Uncle, goodbye." She strode across the small piazza and into her carriage without a glance back.

A few days later Father Riccardi Niccolini arrived to see the pontiff's personal secretary. His large round face seated opposite Giovanni Ciàmpoli glistened with moisture. "Signor Ciàmpoli, I respectfully request your assistance on a most urgent matter. Please give me a definitive response to my question on the imprimatur for Signor Galilei's book. Since he left here last year I have supervised a number of revisions, as suggested by the Holy See, but His Highness the Grand Duke is now putting intolerable pressure on myself, and my family, to complete the task. As you know, the Tuscan ambassador's wife is my niece and families can have a habit of making one's life difficult." Father Riccardi presented an incongruous figure: a giant of a man pleading like a child to a diminutive father.

"Father Riccardi, are you suggesting that your loyalties are being torn between Holy Mother Church, your family and the, I have to say troublesome, Tuscan state?" After his years as private secretary to His Holiness, Giovanni Ciàmpoli had learnt just where to place the emphasis in his questions and comments to ensure the supplicant was entirely in his control. "His Holiness would be most disappointed if he thought that your loyalty to Holy Mother Church wavered for the merest moment. Does the Grand Duke threaten you or your relations with harm?"

"No."

"Does the Grand Duke threaten to remove you from your position as Master of the Sacred Palace?"

"No."

"I see. Does the Grand Duke hold information about you that could threaten your position? Or has he offered you some fine position in his court?"

"No." By now Father Niccolò Riccardi was staring through Giovanni in a state of utter despondency.

"So tell me, what can be so urgent a matter about this book that you do not feel able to resolve it personally? The granting, or otherwise, of an imprimatur for publication in Rome is your responsibility, is it not?"

"Indeed it is, Signor Ciàmpoli. However, it would appear that Signor Galilei now seeks an imprimatur to publish in Florence."

"Fine, then let the Florentines deal with it," snapped Giovanni.

"I am afraid that it will not be quite that simple. I have received word from Father Stefani in Florence that, based on the provisional imprimatur issued by my office, the Florentine Congregation of the Inquisition considers the book suitable for publication. In fact Father Stefani said that he 'was moved to tears at many passages by the humility and reverent obedience displayed by the author.' Father Stefani appears quite excited at the prospective publication of the latest work of our greatest philosopher."

Giovanni added dryly, "Yes, I am sure Father Stefani is a man much given to emotional outbursts during philosophical discussions."

Niccolò did not respond to Giovanni's bait. "However, the provisional imprimatur issued here in Rome does not include the preface and conclusion to the Signor

Galilei's *Dialogue Concerning Two World Systems*. These have been, as I know you to be aware, amended by His Holiness."

Giovanni's patience was now wearing thin, and his room for manoeuvre was shrinking. "If you wish to question the writing of His Holiness you should seek an audience there."

"His Holiness has already been disturbed enough by these sheaves of paper, and of course the dreadful pestilence has slowed all communications between Rome and Florence, transforming routine correspondence into tales of Homeric proportions. Therefore I am asking you to give the order that the imprimatur be issued following His Holiness's amendments. After all, you are close to the mind of His Holiness and, I understand, that of Signor Galilei."

Signor Ciàmpoli stiffened at this impertinent remark. "You dare to claim to understand more than you know. Be warned it is always safer to speak less than you know. How dare you come into my offices and presume so much. I no more know the mind or character of Signor Galilei than that of any other man."

"I am sorry, please excuse my woeful indiscretion, I am at the mercy of your courtesy." Giovanni noticed a glint in Riccardi's eye as he spoke and realized that the Father knew that he had touched something with his previous comment.

Father Ricarrdi seemed somewhat emboldened as he continued to speak. "Signor Ciàmpoli, as your consideration is that this matter should go before His Holiness, perhaps I could humbly accept your advice and ask that an audience be arranged?"

Realizing he had been outmanoeuvred, Giovanni spoke in a more measured, conciliatory tone. "Father Riccardi, perhaps we should take this a little more slowly, so that we may be sure of the best course of action for Holy Mother Church."

"Of course, such delicate matters should be deliberated upon."

"The Florentine Inquisition considers the book worthy of an imprimatur, but they lack the preface and conclusion which have been amended by His Holiness."

"That is precisely so."

"These documents are in your possession, they have been clearly amended and signed by His Holiness?"

"Yes."

"Now tell me, the Florentine Inquisition has the authority to issue an imprimatur?"

"They do indeed, but in a case such as this whereby a work has also been seen and approved by the Vatican, the Florentine Congregation of the Inquisition may be given dispensation to issue a Vatican imprimatur."

"I do not think we need to go quite that far. It seems to me that as the Florentines have done all the work they should also receive the credit for such work. I suggest that you send the preface and conclusion to Florence, inform Father Stefani that we see no reason for the Florentine Inquisition not to proceed with the decision they have reached. We look forward to seeing Signor Galilei's work being published in Florence. Good day to you."

Father Riccardi stood up to leave, and did not conceal his pleasure at this outcome, when Giovanni suddenly spoke again. "Father Riccardi, try not to be in Phaethon's chariot when it crashes to earth."

Father Riccardi left in silence; Giovanni returned to his duties in the pontiff's chambers.

"Where have you been?" asked Pope Urban icily.

"With the Master of the Sacred Palace, Holiness."

"On what business?"

"Father Riccardi was seeking advice in relation to the issuing of an imprimatur for a new work by Signor Galilei."

"I distinctly recall stating that we were to have nothing further to do with that man."

"Yes, Holiness, but…" Giovanni stammered, surprised by the sharpness of the pope's reaction.

"Is not the Master of the Sacred Palace himself entrusted with decisions regarding the issuing of imprimaturs? Are you sure you have not been whispering with Cardinal Borgia or some other Spaniard?" Giovanni tried in vain to interject a response to these accusations. "It seems to me, Giovanni, that you are offering your time and advice in all sorts of quarters except where it is actually required. Here!" Urban shook as he screamed at Giovanni. "You spend more time advising my court than you do me. Where is my advice? Where is my personal secretary? Where is my Giovanni? I'll tell you where, he is busy scheming with the Spaniards. It seems to me that you spend more time in the service of Cardinal Borgia than here in the Holy Office."

Giovanni stood and tried to respond. "Your Holiness, I have no idea from whence such ideas and pernicious lies about me emanate but I can assure you these are lies of the basest kind. I have always been faithful and loyal to you and you alone. Please confront me with my accusers so that I may see their dissembling faces."

The eyes and ears of His Holiness were firmly closed. "Silence. I have already arranged another position for you in Montalto della Marca."

Giovanni could not believe what was happening. "North? To that mountainous wasteland? Up into the war?"

Urban studiously ignored Giovanni's tearful pleas. "You are to take over as governor there no later than next summer. I do not want to see you in the Vatican palaces again; now get out." Giovanni knew Urban well enough to realize that any further attempts to respond would be at best futile and could even be physically dangerous. Pope Urban was beyond reason. In a dazed state of confused anger and disbelief, he took his leave of His Holiness.

2

Father Giustino, as Chief Inquisitor, had every right to be in the long hall of the Vatican secret archive but today he did not have a legitimate reason to be there. A leading member of the Congregation of the Inquisition, he was not beyond procedural and administrative questioning about his presence in the archive. His ears filled with the beat of his heart, and the dry sweet scent of paper and vellum suffused his nostrils, his eyes searched hungrily along the bound volumes and neatly tied packages for the number he sought. When Pope Paul V established the archive he made sure that its existence was widely known but on whom it contained shameful and damming revelations was kept a closely guarded secret. This was the key to its power. To maintain the security of this knowledge and the carefully tended mythology of the archive the volumes and bundles were identified only by a number, with access to the code controlled by the Commissary General's Office. It was not long before Father Giustino found the number he sought: 1181.

He took his hoard of hope and guilt to a small desk below a window. The last addition to the bundle was a report dismissing the anonymous letter he had passed on to Father

Caccini three or four years ago. He felt a small glow of pride at his part in the inclusion of this letter and that it had been taken seriously enough to commission a report. However, his pride immediately moved to anger when he saw that Father Baccarini's mind, even in the last months of his life, had remained sharp and erudite. He leafed though the tiresome adulatory missives on the accession of Urban VIII and correspondence on comets. Then he found the document he hoped to find, and it surpassed all of his expectations. The injunction of 1616 that he and Father Baccarini failed to deliver all those years ago, he couldn't quite bring to the front of his mind the name of the third Father in their company that night. No matter, here was the document ordered by the Commissary General in pristine condition, clearly stating that Signor Galileo Galilei should not hold, teach or defend the Copernican hypothesis. It had not been struck though, it had no marginalia, no note attached explaining the failed delivery, it had not been signed.

Giustino sat gazing at the document allowing its words to drift in and out of focus. The simple existence of this paper decorated with words was of no real consequence at this precise moment in time but, he thought, if Galileo should be brought before the Inquisition, on whatever pretext, this document could be produced to demonstrate that Galileo was clearly guilty of disobeying the Congregation of the Inquisition. The lack of signatures did not present any great difficulty for Father Giustino, he was certain that if the good and eminent men that should have signed it were still alive today they would have no hesitation in correcting such an oversight in defence of Holy Mother Church. He resolved to carry out further investigations so that when the occasion arose this document could be brought to the attention of a commission or inquisitorial court duly signed, where no one would dare to question the memory of the Blessed Eminence Cardinal Bellarmino or Commissary General Seghizzi.

He considered taking the letter out to correct the lack of signatures but decided this could be too much of a risk, better to wait until the time was ripe and he had examined some good examples of the dearly departed signatures. He carefully placed the letter back into the bundle and returned it to the sequence on the shelf. He strode from the archive filled with excitement but with his attention focused on maintaining a suitably calm and sombre demeanour. The destruction of Galileo was certain to lead to the further enhancement of his position.

3

The air was filled with the fecund scents of a summer morning mixed with the slightly musty odour of masonry as Galileo sat, at peace with the world, waiting for Virginia in the courtyard of San Matteo.

"Papa, you should've come after Sext, there is no need for you to be up so early."

"And waste such a beautiful morning. No. Here I have brought some wine for the services, I am sure the Mother Abbess always has a need for decent communion wine. Anyway, I am so tired of those rich clods that pass for students that this good wine, like my fine intellect, is wasted on those fools. It is always a pleasure to engage with a mind that is actually capable of seeing the world. Oh, were that you had been born a boy, you are the best of my pupils and yet imprisoned here."

"Papa, please don't embarrass my position as a bride of Christ."

But nothing could stop his outpouring of pride. "I tell you now, Virginia, you and half of the artisans in Florence would make better mathematicians and philosophers than the idiots I have to give my time to from Court. You allow your mind to interpret your senses; you are not bound by slavish addiction to the bookish authority of the ancients. If there is at least one thing that great dabbler Leonardo was right about, it is that we must trust our senses and not the words of others. Did you know it has actually been said that it was he who originally suggested that the moon did not have its own source of light? Some vicious scandalmonger seems to hang on every corner of my work waiting to try to dampen the brilliance of my discoveries. Mind you, imagine what our intellectual world might be like today if Leonardo had been born a Medici or a Sforza instead of some poor bastard. It seems that great minds are eternally destined to be born into poor pockets, but alas you and I will not change society."

Virginia had heard this particular speech before, but it was not boredom that flattened her voice and distanced her eyes. "Papa, I am afraid that I have some disturbing news for you".

"What? Is you sister unwell?"

"No, papa, it's nothing like that. As you know we have, through your propitious kindness, been blessed with a fine visiting Father. He is a good man and is not unaware of your work and position, indeed he is somewhat sympathetic to your views."

"A monk with a mind, a miracle indeed," said Galileo, laughing.

"Father! Such a comment is unbecoming of you."

"Yes, of course. I am sorry, my dear, please do go on."

"Father Michelotti, before coming to Florence, served at San Francesco al Prato in Perugia. He has recently told me that, three or four summers ago, he saw a man whom he now knows to be Signor delle Colombe deep in conversation with Father Caccini. Although Caccini's venomous ambition is well known, there was no reason for Father Michelotti to think this meeting to be of any particular note. However, now that his is aware of Signor delle Colombe, and the antipathy that exists between you and delle Colombe, Father Michelotti took it upon himself to ask me to inform you of this observation. He has also said that there are rumours travelling from Rome that you have fallen foul from His Holiness's favour. Papa, you need to be more careful than ever."

"Oh, is that all, child? There are no developments here, just a chance meeting, I am sure. Three or four summers past was a lifetime ago and there are always rumours. I am surprised that you should allow them to defile your ears."

"You are, I am sure, absolutely right, but I fear for you papa."

"You well know that His Holiness and I are friends of old, he has even written poetry in praise of my discoveries. He does me great honour... anyway Caccini is but an ignorant monk."

"That may be so, but he has been able to cause you a great deal of trouble. Papa, consider that every time you make a fool of someone you create an enemy," Virginia interjected calmly.

"...and delle Colombe is an intellectual ant." Galileo's thoughts drifted back some twenty years to a banquet at the villa of the Florentine nobleman, and fellow Lincean, Filippo Salviati,

"Any child, any fool indeed, can demonstrate that ice does not float because of its shape, just take a piece of any shape and watch it float. And why does it float? Ice floats because it is rarefied water and thus has a lower specific weight than ordinary water." Signor Salviati's excellent wine cellar contributed a little to the force of Galileo's declamations.

"Leo, please calm yourself, you go too far; the room is not so large that you will not be heard," said his friend and host Filippo.

"Quite so," began Ludovico delle Colombe's quiet retort. "It is clear that Signor Galilei either has not read, or has read but not understood, the words of Aristotle on this matter." Galileo felt his face flush with rage at this jibe, and he was about to launch into a furious response when Duke Cosimo caught his eye and signalled that he remain silent. "He plainly states," continued delle Colombe, "that shape is the determining factor of whether or not a body floats. Ice, says the philosopher that most intellectuals read, is condensed water and thus its particles, as with any other frozen substance, huddle tightly together, so it floats despite being a heavier form of water by virtue of its broad shape. Also, for a further example, if one takes a ball of ebony it will assuredly sink as soon as it is placed in water, whereas a broad chip of ebony will float, again demonstrating that shape is the cause of floating. This is no mystery, one only has to pick up the book and read the words of the greatest philosopher the world has ever known." Ludovico sat back and took a victoriously genteel sip of wine.

Galileo, now calm, responded with forced levity. "I suggest that my friend try wetting his feet in the water of experience, as Archimedes is said to have done, rather than rely solely on the dry words of ancient authority to inform him of the nature of water."

"Well, if we are to allow the words of any fraud into intellectual debate let us call in the kitchen maid," snapped Ludovico.

Galileo's response was immediate and aggressive. "I am sure that the kitchen maid is as honest and pure as the driven snow and has done nothing to allow her name to be maligned thus. At least we could be certain that she would speak from her direct experience of the world rather than simply reading about it." The room exploded in laughter with Galileo, and he rode the wind of humour as Ludovico glowed red. "The kitchen maid will know, by observation, that any piece of ice of indeterminate shape will float. She will also observe that her iron kettle will float, but that it will sink as soon as the air in the kettle is replaced with water. Why is this? Is it because the water adds weight to the kettle? No, because the water in the kettle weighs as much as the water around it. The kettle floats because of the combination of the specific weight of the iron and that of the air in it; the combination of kettle and air has a lower specific weight than the water. Likewise, your ebony chip floats because the air attached to its surface contributes to the overall specific weight, making it less than water." Making exaggerated gestures with his arms Galileo outlined the shapes as he spoke. "If Signor delle Colombe has difficulty understanding any of this perhaps he should spend more time in the kitchen." Everyone present, except Ludovico, was near to tears at Galileo's bravura comic delivery. Ludovico, silent with rage at such impertinence, was saved from responding by Duke Cosimo's intervention.

"Gentlemen, please, this evening's discussion was to be a philosophical debate not a cock fight. I suggest that Signor Galilei put his unusual views in writing so that we may ponder them at our leisure."

"Thank you, Your Highness, I would be most pleased to do so."

Puffed up with pride, Galileo lifted his glass and glanced around the room soaking up the laughter, applause and the Duke's approval. Ludovico shrank into his seat.

The sound of Virginia's voice brought Galileo back to San Matteo. "Papa, I am sorely afraid that there are those who would wish to do you great harm with this new book of yours."

"Dearest daughter, I am greatly succoured at your concern for an old man but believe me when I say that these rumours are no more than lies, probably initiated by jealous Jesuits. His Holiness and I are more than friends, he understands the value of my work and would not jeopardize it." Virginia opened her mouth to speak but Galileo raised his hand to silence her. "Before you say anything that hints at a conspiracy, you must realize that His Holiness was simply too busy to see me during my last visit to Rome. Don't forget, dear, we are still at war. As for Father Riccardi's delay in issuing my imprimatur, the Master of the Scared Palace ha! He probably has difficulty deciding with which hand to wipe his backside."

"Father, please mind your tongue. You should not abuse a servant of Holy Mother Church thus."

"No, of course not. Anyway, none of this is of any consequence since the plague has once more brought the country to a standstill but keeps Madam Fortune busy. God willing we will survive this pestilence." He held his daughter's hand and in a quieter, more conciliatory tone, continued: "I am an old man, I have one eye devoid of light and my breath leaves me without warning, what possible threat could I be to anyone? And, I have decided to abandon trying to have my book published in Rome, I cannot risk having the manuscript destroyed by some efficiently eager quarantine official. I will try instead to gain permission from the Florentine Congregation of the Inquisition for an imprimatur."

"Papa dear, I beg your forgiveness for speaking bluntly, but I believe this course of action is both unwise and dangerous. If you must press this book on the world, at least go back to Venice where you may be offered some protection."

"A father might think his daughter did not love him, trying to drive him to distant cities," said Galileo with mock sadness.

"Papa, do not jest about the Congregation of the Inquisition."

"Darling daughter, do not fear for me. The Dominicans have had their day of glory at my expense and it was they that failed in the end."

"Very well, papa, but please indulge me in one last painful comment on this subject." Galileo assented. Virginia studied the flagstones and her feet as she spoke.

"As you know, my brother Vincenzio spends a great deal of his time trying to engage himself with Court and..." He stared intently at her as she searched desperately for the right phrase. "In short, papa, a son who has no relation to his father may be an unwitting risk to the father. I know you have tried desperately to be a proud father to Cenzo but..."

Galileo slumped into the stone seat his hand slipping from hers. "I see. Has he..."

"No, I do not believe he would ever knowingly betray you." They sat in sad silence for some time before Galileo found himself able to speak, his voice struggling in his throat.

"Cenzo may give me little cause for pride but I am sure he has no malice towards me. However, you are quite right, a father should be mindful of a son. I think I should go now."

Galileo shuffled away from the convent, his feet barely parting from the ground. Virginia watched his wretched figure move down the track, tears flowed freely down her face at the pity she felt for her father but she felt anger, regret and guilt at herself. Vincenzio hardly registered in her thoughts at all.

Galileo left the track and wandered aimlessly through the groves of orange and fig trees. Cenzo? He thought. Surely not. No, never. His son would not betray him, even by accident. He considered Vincenzo to be a fool in constant need of money but not so that he would act against his own blood. But then doubts crept into his mind; perhaps a craven idiot such as Cenzo could innocently betray the Good Lord Himself, but he has no malice. The son must be mindful of the father, he resolved to be a more attentive father and invite Cenzo to live at *il Gioiello*. He then recalled that Vincenzo was quick to reject the position offered by His Holiness, he asked himself if he could have had some other more lucrative offer? As Galileo walked he was unaware of the world around him, by turns he wanted to wretch or burst into tears; his heart pounded and slowed, he broke into an intense sweat and then felt cold.

For days after he hardly left his bedchamber, spoke to Maria or ate the food she prepared for him. Eventually, almost out of boredom, he returned to flicking idly through his notes. His interest in presenting to the world his view of the shape of the universe returned, but at unexpected moments he found that tears of grief fought with anger as his mind whirled involuntarily towards his son, Marina the mother of his children, and that demon of shadows and pain, the past. Slowly, he convinced himself that worrying about his relationship with Vincenzio was not a good enough reason to keep his own brilliance hidden, no matter what the cost.

4

Ludovico stood in the shade of the portico of the Pantheon and, much to his surprise, found that he was disappointed by the new surroundings of his beloved iconic building. Where the previous squalor had given something for the dome to rise above, it was now dwarfed and imprisoned by the bombastic palazzos of the *nouveaux riches*. The greatness of the past forgotten, it had become a mere bauble to be gazed upon from the walls of windows that enclosed the ancient building. It was with a heavy but determined heart that he made the short walk in the June heat, on unsteady legs, past sopra Minerva to the Collegio Romano.

Ludovico felt old for a man in his late fifties, he doubted that he would see another spring. He entered the left-hand portal of the Collegio and struggled up the stone stairs to the study of Monsignor Paolo Febei, deaf to the chatter and movement of students around him. Father Caccini had already arrived, he introduced Ludovico and a slightly unseemly shuffle took place to accommodate the new arrival in the tiny room. For the first time during their long confederacy, Ludovico saw Father Caccini in a plain habit, a sign, he thought, of Caccini's discomfort at attending a meeting in the very heart of the Society of Jesus. The three men sat in an awkward silence for a little while: Monsignor Febei tried to appear in control from the commanding position of his desk but Father Caccini spoke first.

"Gentlemen. I think we are all only too well aware of the delicacy and importance of our shared concerns about the condition of knowledge being taught in our institutions, and the threat posed to them by certain attempts to introduce 'new' knowledge. Furthermore, the position taken by the Holy See on these matters appears to be less than clear." The other men nodded their agreement but neither spoke, each assessing the stranger opposite. "I think I can speak for all of us when I say that we have been given some hope, now that a sharp and poisonous thorn has been removed from the softest parts of our flesh and returned to Florence." The other two men grinned and snorted involuntarily, the tension in the room vanished in a puff of humour. "So, shall we put aside our court ball manners and take to the subject in hand?"

Monsignor Febei replied, smiling warmly. "Father Caccini, Signor delle Colombe; may I call you Ludovico? Thank you. You both have the advantage over me in that you both know the Florentine mathematician personally, whereas I know him only by reputation. Perhaps you could give me a little of his person?"

A brief glance between Ludovico and Father Caccini was all that was required for Ludovico to offer his pen portrait of the man with whom he had duelled verbally on so many occasions, always coming off the worse. "Signor Galilei writes, as he speaks, with the gutter tongue of the common man; he makes no effort to raise his disputes to the scholarly language of thought, as used throughout the centuries by the great authorities. Indeed, I believe he does this for the sole purpose of being able to colour his disputations with the profanities of the tavern. I shall never understand how, given his refusal to engage the tongue of scholarly dispute, he has ever managed to be taken seriously. And yet he manages to threaten us all."

"Yes, Ludovico, I can see clearly how you have been wronged by this man but, if I may play the part of the Devil's advocate, what is the greater risk he poses, beyond that of personal insult?"

"Monsignor Febei, before his untimely death, I had the good fortune to spend some time discussing this very matter with his Blessed Eminence Cardinal Bellarmino, may the souls of the faithful departed rest in eternal peace." A gentle "Amen" drifted about the room on the iridescent dust of late afternoon. "Cardinal Bellarmino and I shared this single concern: if this man is allowed to continue publishing his heretical and anti-Aristotelian works, he is in effect being allowed to undermine the very foundations of our intellectual and educational establishments. Given that our universities and schools teach the works of Aristotle as much as they propound Holy Mother Church's exegesis of the Holy Bible, if they are mocked and made to look foolish in one arena this will surely influence their authority, in the eyes of the common man, in the other arena. I speak now not as an intellectual who may see through these vain disputes but from the perspective of the ordinary man who is not capable of subtle thought and will simply see the cornerstone of state made to appear as worthless as a jesters jape." Exhausted by the effort of his summary, Ludovico fell silent, his point made he invited no questions.

"Beautifully put, Ludovico, you are clearly aware of the significant role of education within the Society of Jesus, and its function as a bulwark in the defence of Holy Mother Church against those that would attempt to assert spurious rights to Biblical interpretation. I offer you my heartfelt gratitude for all that you have done in this war without desire of profit or thanks. You are indeed a true defender of the Faith and Truth. However, I am a little puzzled by the role of the Dominican Congregation of the Inquisition, how is this man allowed to flourish thus? Perhaps, Father Caccini, you could give us the benefit of a Dominican perspective on this business?"

Father Caccini's response did not rise to the taunt that the Domincans alone had failed Holy Mother Church in the Galileo matter. "Monsignor Febei, you have raised a question that has left me speechless for more years than I care to recall. Signor Galilei seems to have led a charmed life in his relations with the Curia but I believe that could change." Caccini paused until he was sure he had the Monsignor's full attention. "Like my honoured friend Signor delle Colombe, I too was favoured by the Lord to spend some time discussing these matters with the Blessed Cardinal Bellarmino. I will not pretend to have known him as an intimate, but I am confident that if he were here now he would be advising us to put aside petty historical grievances." Father Caccini paused again, this time for effect. "Cardinal Bellarmino was a modest man of profound faith, he would, I am certain, say to us now: 'You call yourself a Dominican, a Jesuit, an academic. These distinctions are meaningless in the fight for Truth and the right to uphold the Revealed Truth of the authority of Holy Mother Church.' I confess that in years past I had hoped to improve my position within Holy Mother Church by exposing Galileo but I now realize that there is no better advancement or reward than to defend our most Holy Church." Caccini spoke with force and commitment, but as Ludovico listened he suspected that in the darker recesses of his mind Father Caccini still clung to the hope of further recognition.

With the confident air of a man in authority, Monsignor Febei pronounced his thoughts. "I am moved and honoured by the declarations of Faith by you, whom I hope to be able to call friends. You are both obviously already aware of my views on the writings of Signor Galilei, but in order to reciprocate your bold honesty I will now give voice to them. I, like you, Ludovico, am deeply disturbed at the possible damage Signor Galilei's writings could inflict on our educational institutions. I am in no position to say whether or not I consider him to be a heretic but there is no doubt in my mind that he has the potential to create untold harm and damage if he is allowed to continue, unchecked, to undermine the Aristotelian foundations of our noble educational institutions. He must be stopped. So, how should we proceed? Indeed, do we actually need to take any action at all? After all, it is no secret that he came to Rome seeking an imprimatur for his new book but failed miserably in achieving his goal."

Ludovico responded first. "That may be so, but I can tell you, after many years of dealing with this man, he does not give up easily. I can assure you he will continue to seek an imprimatur by any means at his disposal."

Father Caccini concurred with delle Colombe's observation. "My friend Ludovico speaks the truth, he will not rest until he has got his work in print. I can also say that I am aware that when Galileo was last in Rome he made several requests to meet with his friend, His Beatitude himself but was refused an audience. However, I would not read too much into this small detail, as I am also aware that His Holiness has personally made suggestions with regard to revisions to his text so that it may be published. But providence has provided us with a little more time, with the recent death of Prince Cesi the Accadèmia dei Lincei is now in such disarray that it could not find its way to publishing a caterer's inventory, so I doubt that they will attempt to publish a new philosophical work of any kind."

"So when – as it does not appear that we can rely on 'if' – so when Signor Galilei is given permission to publish, are we to understand that it may take him some while to find funding and a printer willing to carry out the task?" asked Monsignor Febei.

"Yes, that is so," replied Father Caccini. "Furthermore, if he has the support of His Holiness I do not see how we can stop the publication of this book once he has the necessary permission. Ludovico do you have any other information from Florence that may be of use?"

Ludovico jerked forward, startled; he had been drifting from the discussion. "What? No. I have already told you everything I know of this book and you are unable to do anything."

Monsignor Febei tried a softer approach to Ludovico. "Perhaps there are some other, apparently minor, scraps of information that seem irrelevant or unimportant that we may have another view on?" Febei spoke with the soothing tones of a man well versed in extracting just the right irrelevancies.

Ludovico mechanically recounted the information he had, and as an afterthought added, "Oh, one of my students befriended Vincenzio Galilei and, for a small fee, was willing to draw whatever information he could from him, which was precious little as I gather father and son are barely on speaking terms. But he did mention something about Spain."

At the mention of Spain, Monsignor Febei almost leapt out of his chair. "My dear Ludovico, this could be far more important than you can imagine. Please, I beg you to search your mind."

Ludovico was surprised by the Monsignor's response. "Um, er, now... It seems that our friend has been corresponding with the Spanish Admiralty. I think he claimed to have found a method for measuring longitude at sea and, of course, he wanted a king's ransom for it without providing any proof. This is yet another one of his lies, such as his claim to have invented the telescope; utter rubbish of course. But one has to acknowledge that he is a genius of self promotion: profit not discovery drives this charlatan." Monsignor Febei gently probed Ludovico for more detail. "I do not know by what minor miracle he hoped to deliver longitude to the Spaniards but they were obviously not convinced by him either. However, there is absolutely no doubt that the first captain to be able to measure longitude will not only rule the seas but will, I am sure, find the routes to great wealth."

"I see. Friends, there exists within the Curia a struggle for power and influence, this much is an open secret, but what you may not realize is that the force for change in this game of wills is the Spanish Collegiate of Cardinals led by his Eminence Gasparo Borgia. His Holiness is extremely unhappy about this situation and is having to work furiously behind the scenes to maintain the status quo within the Curia and keep the Spaniards under control. I am confident that if His Holiness were aware of Signor Galilei's correspondence with the Spanish Admiralty the effect on their relationship would be quite dramatic." Febei sat back smiling to himself.

"Do you think he would be angry enough to prevent the publication of what will surely be another of Galileo's anti-Aristotelian tracts?" Ludovico asked optimistically.

"Who can say? The beauty of this kind of information is that it is very likely to have something of the effect we require without having to be demonstrated: simply being tainted by the Spanish brush will have some impact on Signor Galilei, I assure you."

"Let us assume then," said Father Caccini, "that Galilei is pushed into great disfavour by this information and his book is not published, then what?"

Febei and Ludovico looked blank. "I do not understand your question," Ludovico said. "Surely if Galileo's books are not published we have succeeded in our task?"

"To an extent yes. But he will write other books. We need to find a way to stop him for good?"

Monsignor Febei shuffled uncomfortably. "What are you suggesting?"

"Oh, Monsignor, have no fear. Like you, I do not believe that an evil act may be justified even by the removal of an evil. I just wonder if there may be some other more permanent solution?"

"Father Caccini, take a care, we both wear the cloth of the Church," warned Monsignor Febei.

Caccini continued without concern. "Galileo has left Rome empty-handed, he will most assuredly continue in his efforts to gain an imprimatur. So, perhaps we should consider an alternative to prohibition? I am only thinking aloud, but what if we were to help him get his book printed legitimately? If, for example, I were able to get a word or two into the ears of certain members of the Florentine Congregation of the Inquisition we may be able to expedite the publication of Signor Galilei's book through the granting of an imprimatur in Florence." Caccini preened himself involuntarily as he spoke. "I have some influence with Father Stefani in Florence. Galileo's book will almost certainly be a controversial work requiring an expert view from a commission, a commission drawn from this very establishment. Indeed, Monsignor Febei, you may even be invited to join such a commission. In addition," Father Caccini drew a long breath, as if deciding whether to continue: "I am aware of the existence of certain documents which, if Galileo should find himself before the Inquisition, could put an end to his mischief for good. And this Spanish connection may aid us in the introduction of the Inquisition."

"My dear Caccini, you should have been a cardinal. Is it not indeed ironic that our work today in silencing a man of letters in defence of Holy Mother Church will not be recorded? History will not know us, or our part in the salvation of the minds of men. We have only the gratitude and certainty of our faith for our reward. Such a bold and ambitious plan, do you believe it will silence Signor Galilei?" asked Monsignor Febei.

"Who can say?" replied Father Caccini casually.

5

"Monsignor Febei, Your Holiness." Pope Urban did not look up from the architectural drawings spread out before him as he spoke.

"Ah, Monsignor Febei. Architects, they are both wonderfully simple and hateful, are they not?" He spoke with bright enthusiastic vigour, without waiting for Monsignor Febei to formally present himself.

"As you wish, Holiness," replied Febei uncertainly.

"Yes. We give them a commission, they produce a design, it is approved and it is built. A beautifully simple relationship, but then comes the sting:" the Pope now looked up, directly at the Monsignor. "They will never give a straight answer as to the cost of their design. But then disputes over money are not in themselves complex, unlike philosophical disputes." Returning his gaze to the drawing, Urban asked, "So has the commission made its findings about Signor Galilei's new book?"

"Indeed we have, Your Holiness." Ever since word had spread about the Ciàmpoli incident the previous year, all visitors to His Holiness maintained a greater than usual distance of response.

"Good. So please enlighten me."

"The commission found a number of technical faults in relation to the book's production with which I will not bore Your Beatitude. Signor Galilei sets out to discuss what he terms 'two world systems' in the form of a dialogue; in effect he describes two possible shapes of the universe, the Sun at the centre of one and, the accepted view, that the Earth is at the centre of the universe. He claims to treat each equally, neither favouring nor disfavouring one model over the other, but the commission did not find this to be the case. The commission is of the opinion that Signor Galilei not only teaches and defends the immobility or rest of the Sun at the centre of the universe, around which both planets and the earth revolve with their own motions, as originally described in the banned book of Copernicus, but also that he is suspected of firmly adhering to this opinion, and indeed that he holds to this view. If I may? I might direct Your Holiness to the finely detailed report of Monsignor Inchofer on this matter."

" Good, Inchofer is an astute man. I cannot say I am surprised to hear any of this. Leo –" Urban's mouth suddenly slammed shut, and with a faint smile he continued. "Signor Galilei has never known when to stop and be silent. But I sense that you have more to say."

"Yes, Your Holiness." Febei faltered.

"Well? Why do you halt mid-tale?" asked Urban, vainly attempting to conceal the irritation in his voice and brushing the drawings aside.

"What I have to say is extremely difficult and sensitive in its nature, Holiness, if I may be permitted to speak freely?"

The pontiff replied with soft encouragement. "Of course, we are all only ever interested in the truth and the protection of Holy Mother Church. Now, please go on."

"In this dialogue, Signor Galilei puts each description into a different mouth so that they may dispute their views. The new, Sun-centred view he puts into the mouth of an erudite nobleman, believed by some members of the commission to be based on one of his Florentine supporters. The orthodox view, the fine words of Aristotle and many other great scholars, he puts into the mouth of a fool; indeed he even calls him by the name of Simplicio."

"I see, he sets out to ridicule our great establishments."

"Furthermore, Your Most Blessed Beatitude, some members of the commission felt that in creating this Simplicio he was also aiming to ridicule you personally."

Pope Urban froze with rage. With some difficulty and without further enquiry he whispered his response to this revelation. "You are to take these findings to the Commissary General immediately. I will issue orders that all further production of this book shall cease, that all unsold copies are destroyed and that Signor Galilei is to be tried by the Congregation of the Inquisition here in Rome."

With some hesitation, Monsignor Febei asked, "Yes, Your Holiness, but...but what about the Duke?"

"There is nothing to worry about there, the Medicis are a spent force; he would not dare to challenge Holy Mother Church in this matter. I want you to inform the Commissary General that Signor Galilei is to be prosecuted with the full weight of the law. I shall entrust you to ensure that adequate charges are brought so that he does not wriggle away this time, including the use of those boring technical irregularities you mentioned. Our feet are quite wet enough with the waters from Galilee."

"If Your Holiness permits it, may I make a further observation?"

"Please do, I find your efficiency in this matter most refreshing, Monsignor Febei."

"Thank you, Your Holiness. I understand that a trial by the Congregation of the Inquisition would involve the Holy Tribunal, and that Cardinal Borgia is likely to be a member of the Tribunal?"

"Of course, what of it?"

"Well, it may be nothing, Holiness, but I understand that Signor Galilei has been in correspondence with the Spanish Admiralty. And…"

Urban silenced Febei with a slightly raised hand, there were other ears in the room. "I see. Thank you, I shall take a particular interest in Cardinal Borgia's position in this case." With a flick of the wrist Monsignor Febei was dismissed, he made a gently dignified but hurried exit.

6

The wind whipped around the courtyard of San Matteo. Galileo and Virginia huddled close together.

"Papa, it is so cold, please let us go inside. The refectory is still decorated for the Nativity of our Blessed Lord, and it looks quite lovely – come, I'll show you." Virginia's voice trembled with the cold.

"No, I want us to stay here on 'our' bench." Galileo spoke with a distantly firm tone; the wind drew water from his eyes. "I need you to be strong for all of us now." Virginia's mouth opened with a question but Galileo stopped its release. "Please just listen. I had hoped matters would not get to this stage, but they have. I leave tomorrow for Rome."

He couldn't stop her this time. "What? Papa, no, you can't, you're too old, too ill, the plague... No, Papa, you must stay here."

He wrapped his arm around her and smothered her crackling voice and moist cheeks in his shoulder. "Shh, shh. I must go. I was summoned to the Inquisition in Rome about two months ago; I have put them off this long but if I do not go now they will send soldiers to arrest me. I have written to doctors and nobles and prelates, all to no avail. Now, in my moment of greatest need, my noble friends avert their gaze. His Highness the Duke has provided me with a litter for the journey, and I shall travel in small easy stages."

"Why?" asked the forlorn voice muffled in his shoulder.

"I don't know, the Inquisition works on the assumption that the accused knows what he is guilty of. It can only be my new book. Orders were sent out to cease publication and confiscate all copies, but fortunately Signor Landini had already sold them all. As we sit here, dear, my words are travelling across Europe." They sat in huddled silence for a while. "I don't want you to worry yourself sick about this, I am confident I have a good case to answer them and will be back before the summer. After all, I have the appropriate imprimaturs, the letter from Cardinal Bellarmino, the support of His Holiness. This is all the mistake of some idiot nitpicking cleric, you'll see. But I am old and it is a long journey. If…" His voice was now cracking. "If anything should happen to me during my travels, I have given Maria instructions on how to proceed, but I need you to have a care for Livia and Cenzo." Virginia's grip tightened as he spoke. "I have also written to Signor Diodati in Paris with respect to future publications should the need arise." His voice finally collapsed.

"Venice! Papa, Venice. You could escape to Venice, please I beg you to go." Virginia shouted in pitiful hopefulness, pushing her face up to his. "You know the Doge will give you safe harbour."

"No. If I go to Venice I am certain to be found guilty of something in absentia and I am too close to death to risk excommunication. I can show them I am right and have acted only out of faith in Our Lord; everything will be fine," he said, his voice misplacing its sincerity.

7

"So, it took me two weeks of picking my way around towns and hamlets, avoiding bandits, the pestilence and freezing to death; here I am."

"Well I'm glad you came through it safely, Leo. I just wish the circumstances were better." Caterina's voice had lost none of its soothing softness since Galileo had last visited. Francesco shuffled slightly in his chair, and made several attempts to speak before actually doing so.

"Yes, Leo, we're just so pleased you're safe and in good health. And er... Well, I'm afraid this is a little awkward."

"Francesco, don't be so rude to our honoured guest, if you have something to say, say it," demanded Caterina.

"I have received instruction from His Highness the Duke to cooperate with the Holy See in any practicable manner. And, well, the Congregation of the Inquisition, which is to say His Holiness, have stipulated that you remain here under house arrest; visitors are to be strictly limited." Francesco snatched up his wine.

"How ridiculous, and what does the Holy See imagine Leo is likely to do? I wonder what could have been done to prevent this situation becoming so horrible?" Caterina shot Francesco an angry, fiery glance as she spoke.

"No, please, Caterina, this is quite all right, I expected as much," interjected Galileo quietly. "Indeed, I am aware that my very presence in your home may cause you some difficulties and embarrassment, for which I can only apologize and express my deepest gratitude at your kindnesses. And believe me, I would rather be under house arrest here, with the beautiful Caterina, than in the cells of Castel Sant' Angelo. And it will be much easier for me to travel to the den of my inquisitors from here in Palazzo Firenze than it would be from Villa Medici. I am confident that this whole business will be sorted out quickly and we can return to our lives."

"I am comforted and honoured by your understanding of the delicacy of the situation." Francesco spoke with noticeable relief. "But alas, I am afraid that Caterina and I will be often engaged at Villa Medici looking after a Spanish painter to whom the Duke insists we offer full ambassadorial courtesies, though why His Highness should commission a Spaniard when there are so many fine Tuscan painters to choose from is a mystery to me."

Galileo replied softly, without a hint of disappointment. "My dear friends, wherever our heads may lie I know that your kindness is always near me. I wonder, dear Caterina, if I could prevail upon your kindness a little further?"

"Of course, Leo, anything that is within my power," Caterina replied warmly.

"My daughter, Virginia, is likely to be in correspondence with your estimable highness whilst I am here in Rome. It is my wish that, when you provide her with the news she will assuredly crave, you do so in the most positive fashion that honour permits. There will be no need, for instance, to overburden her with the dull daily details of this business." The plea in Galileo's voice was quite unnecessary.

"I understand perfectly, Leo, and of course I will do my best to furnish your charming daughter with such information as appears pertinent, without causing her undue distress." Caterina wrapped her arm through Galileo's and gripped firmly as she spoke.

"Thank you."

Two interminable months passed before Galileo heard the strident steps of a group of soldiers cross the courtyard of Palazzo Firenze, on a dark, grey, April morning. No words were exchanged. He had been prepared for this morning since he began his journey to Rome. Despite the gloom, the damp and the cold, the streets were uncomfortably busy for Galileo as he was marched along the Via della Scrofa and around the Pantheon to Piazza Minerva.

He was led to the left of the bare, imposing façade of Santa Maria sopra Miverva, to a modest doorway jammed into the corner of the piazza; the entrance to the Dominican convent, which also houses the offices of the Congregation of the Inquisition. Although Galileo had walked across this piazza many times during his trips to Rome he could not recall ever seeing this door open. As they approached, the door opened, apparently of its own volition, and he passed through the doorway noting wryly that this building bore the same number as his own home *Il Gioiello*: 42. Perhaps that was a good omen, he thought. Within a few feet of passing through the portal they were moving leftwards across a cloister, and he was soon standing in a plain white room, about eight metres long by three with a barrel-vaulted ceiling; two desks with chairs were placed near the end wall, a single chair faced them. The soldiers motioned him to sit in the solitary chair, then they stood a little behind him and they all waited. The poor light of a grim day leached into the room from four windows to his left, the faint shadow from the windows placing barely perceptible bars on the floor at the prisoner's feet. Galileo began to tremble as the damp and cold began to reach into his bones.

His military escort had changed duty twice, always in silence, before the inquisitors made their entrance: two men in the black habits of the Dominican Order took their positions at the two desks. As the inquisitors entered, the guards jabbed Galileo in the shoulders, by way of instruction to stand. He fought the urge to shout out about being kept waiting, indeed he did his best to appear unperturbed by the whole business by standing calmly, firmly and trying to appear resolutely unconcerned, but his seventy winters got the better of him and he felt old and frail.

The more senior-looking Dominican at last spoke, his voice dispassionate and dismissive: "You may be seated. Galileo Galilei, you have been summoned to appear personally here in Rome at the palace of the Holy Office, the quarters of the Reverend Father Commissary, fully in the presence of the Commissary General, Reverend Father Vincenzio Maculano of Firenzuola." He placed his outspread hand lightly on his chest as he spoke, indicating that this was he; the other man remained silent and motionless. He continued, "and of his assistant Reverend Father Carlo Sinceri, Prosecutor of the Holy Office." He gestured towards the other man. Galileo was then invited to take an oath to speak only the truth in the sight of God. He complied.

After a brief series of questions confirming Galileo's identity and how he came to Rome, Father Maculano came straight to the meat of the matter. A book was passed to Galileo, which he confirmed was indeed the book he had most recently written. "Yes, this is my *Dialogue Concerning the Two Chief World Systems*, a book written by me in dialogue form that treats the constitution of the world and the arrangement of the heavens and the elements. I know this book very well: it is one of those printed in Florence. I acknowledge it as mine and written by me." The pride in Galileo's voice seemed to energize the rest of his tired body.

Father Maculano appeared pleased with Galileo's answer. "When and where was this book composed, and how long did it take to write?" he asked.

Galileo responded without hesitation. "In regard to the place, I composed it in Florence, beginning ten or twelve years ago; and it must have taken me seven or eight years to write, but not continuously."

There was a long pause while Father Maculano checked his notes and those of Father Sinceri. "Have you been in Rome at other times, especially in the year 1616, and for what occasion?" he asked casually, without looking up.

Galileo was taken aback by this sudden change of direction. He sat in silence for some moments then spoke with a faltering staccato voice. "I was in Rome in 1616; then I was here in the... second year of His Holiness Urban the Eighth's pontificate; and lastly I was here three years ago, the occasion being that I sought an imprimatur to have my book printed." He thought for some time before continuing; he decided to try to confront the likely attack of his questioners before some trap was set for him. "The occasion for my being in Rome in the year 1616 was that, having heard objections to Nicolaus Copernicus's opinion of the Earth's motion, the sun's stability, and the arrangement of the heavenly spheres, in order to be sure of holding only holy and Catholic opinions, I came to hear what was proper to hold in regard to this topic."

"Did you come to Rome of your own accord or were you summoned?" Maculano barked, "and for what reason were you summoned, and with which person or persons did you discuss these topics?"

Galileo's composure left him, he straightened in the chair, slammed his hands down on the arms and shouted, "In 1616 I came to Rome of my own accord, I was not summoned!" He took a few moments to regain his breath, and injected a hint of apology into his voice. "In Rome I discussed these matters with some Cardinals who oversaw the Holy Office at that time, most especially with Cardinals Bellarmino, Aracoli, San Eusebio, Bonsi and, I think, Cardinal d'Ascoli."

"What specifically did you discuss with these Cardinals of the Holy Office?"

"The occasion for discussing with the said cardinals was that they wanted to be informed about Copernicus's doctrine, his book being very difficult to understand for those who are not professional mathematicians and astronomers. In particular they wanted to understand the arrangement of the heavenly spheres according to Copernicus's hypothesis, how he places the sun at the centre of the planet's orbits, how around the sun he places next the orbit of Venus…" Galileo felt that he was now in safe territory, that he was well supported by the Cardinals he referred to and he proceeded to lecture his inquisitors on Copernican astronomy.

Father Maculano was, however, more interested in the details of Galileo's conversations in Rome than his expertise and opinions on astronomy. "Since you came to Rome to be able to have the resolution and truth regarding…" Father Maculano consulted his notes once more, "…objections to Nicolaus Copernicus's opinion… What was decided about this matter?"

Galileo wanted to say, "You know the answer to that, you fool," but managed to restrain himself. "Regarding the controversy that centred on the above-mentioned opinion of the Sun's stability and the Earth's motion, it was decided by the Holy Congregation of the Index that this opinion, taken absolutely, is repugnant to Holy Scripture and is to be admitted only hypothetically in the way Copernicus takes it."

"Were you informed of this decision, and if so by whom?" Malucano asked; Father Sinceri seemed particularly attentive at this point.

"I was indeed notified of the said decision of the Congregation of the Index, personally by Lord Cardinal Bellarmino." Galileo's confidence was growing at the mention of his powerful supporter.

"What, precisely, did the Most Eminent Cardinal Bellarmino tell you about the said decision? Did he say anything else on the matter, and if so what?" Maculano placed his questions like pieces on a chessboard, preparing to checkmate his opponent.

Galileo sensed his own victory in this ridiculous game. "Lord Cardinal Bellarmino told me that Copernicus's opinion could be held hypothetically, as Copernicus himself had held it. His Eminence knew that I held it hypothetically, namely in the way that Copernicus held it, as you can see from an answer by the same Lord Cardinal in a letter to Father Master Paolo Antonio Foscarini, Provincial of the Carmelites. I have a copy of this, and in it one finds these words: 'I say that it seems to me that Your Paternity and Signor Galilei are proceeding prudently by limiting yourselves to speaking hypothetically and not absolutely.' This letter by the said Lord Cardinal is dated 12 April 1615. Moreover, His Eminence told me that even if taken absolutely this opinion could be neither held nor defended."

"You saw his Eminence the Lord Cardinal Bellarmino in February 1616?" Galileo nodded. "What, precisely, was decided and made known to you during this discourse?"

Galileo shuddered at the recollection of that evening. "Lord Cardinal Bellarmino told me that since Copernicus's opinion, taken absolutely, was contrary to Holy Scripture, it could be neither held nor defended, but it could be taken and used hypothetically. In conformity with this, I keep a certificate by Lord Cardinal Bellarmino himself, dated 26 May 1616, in which he says that Copernicus's opinion cannot be held or defended, being against Holy Scripture. I present a copy of this certificate. I have retained the original and have it with me here in Rome." He passed the letter to Father Sinceri, and sat back feeling quite satisfied.

Father Maculano did not look at the letter but continued with his questions. "This may be entered into evidence and marked *B*. When these matters were discussed with Lord Cardinal Bellarmino were there any others present, and if so who?"

Galileo shuffled. "When Lord Cardinal Bellarmino notified me of these matters regarding Copernicus's opinion, there were some Dominican Fathers present but I did not know them nor have I seen them since."

Maculano now moved in for the checkmate. "At that time, in the presence of those Fathers were you given an injunction either by them or someone else concerning the same matter?"

Perplexed by this question, Galileo struggled for a response. "As I recall it, the affair took place in the following manner. Lord Cardinal Bellarmino sent for me, and he told me that Copernicus's opinion could not be held or defended, being contrary to Holy Scripture. I do not recall whether these Dominican Fathers were there at first or came afterward; nor do I recall whether they were present when the Lord Cardinal told me that the said opinion could not be held." In growing desperation, he added, "Finally, it may be that I was given an injunction not to hold or defend the said opinion, but I do not recall it since this is something of many years ago."

Father Sinceri produced a document from a Vatican file marked 1181 and read its content aloud. When Sinceri had finished reading the 1616 injunction to Galileo, Father Maculano added, "This document, signed and witnessed by the Lord Cardinal Bellarmino and Commissary General Father Seghizzi, clearly states that you may not in any way whatsoever hold, defend, or teach the opinion of Copernicus. Now do you recall the injunction?"

The shock of this revelation stunned Galileo, then panic began to claw its way through his mind. He was barely able to breathe, the world shrank around him and all he could see were the faint prison bars at his feet. "I do not recall that this injunction was given to me in any other way than orally by Lord Cardinal Bellarmino. I do remember that the injunction was that I could not hold or defend, and maybe even that I could not teach. I do not recall that there was the phrase 'in any way whatsoever'." He began to shrink into the chair, his eyes closed as he continued. "But maybe there was; in fact, I did not think about it or keep it in mind, having received a few months thereafter Lord Cardinal Bellarmino's certificate dated 26 May, which I have presented and in which is explained the order given to me not to hold or defend the said opinion. Regarding the other two phrases in the said injunction now mentioned, namely 'not to teach' and 'in any way whatsoever', I did not retain this in my memory. I think because they are not contained in the said certificate, which I relied upon and kept as a reminder." He fell silent, drained.

Father Maculano ignored Galileo's obvious distress. "After the issuing of this injunction," holding up the document that Father Sinceri had read aloud, "did you obtain permission to write the book earlier identified by yourself?"

Galileo responded wearily. "No. I did not seek permission to write the book, because I did not think that by writing this book I was in any way contradicting the injunction given to me not to hold, defend or teach the said opinion, but rather that I was refuting it."

"Did you obtain permission to print the book and if so from whom? And was this for yourself or someone else?"

Galileo managed to rally some energy for a spirited response. "I should like to have it noted that I turned down many profitable offers to have this book printed in France, Germany and Venice. I came to Rome three years ago to place the book in the hands of the chief censor, the Master of the Sacred Palace, giving him absolute authority to add, delete and change as he saw fit." He then described in detail the protracted process and reasons for eventually acquiring the imprimatur in Florence.

In a slightly bored tone, Father Maculano asked, "When you sought the permission of the Master of the Sacred Palace to print this book, did you reveal to the said Most Reverend Father Master the injunction previously given to you concerning the directive of the Holy Congregation mentioned earlier?"

Like a man washed up from a shipwreck, Galileo barely had the breath to answer. "When I asked the Master of the Sacred Palace for permission to print the book, I did not say anything about the injunction because I did not judge it necessary to tell the Most Reverend Father, because the book neither holds nor defends the opinion of the Earth's motion and the Sun's stability. On the contrary, I show in my book that Copernicus's reasons are invalid and inconclusive."

"So, you did not inform the Master of the Sacred Palace of the existence of this injunction when you sought an imprimatur?"

"No," groaned Galileo.

Without warning or further explanation, Father Maculano suddenly announced, "That concludes the proceedings for today." At this, Galileo sat up, expecting to be marched back to Palazzo Firenze. "Signor Galilei, you would ordinarily be taken from here and held in the prison of Castel Sant' Angelo until the time of your next deposition." The little energy Galileo had mustered now left him. "However, given your age and infirmity it has been decided that you will be held under house arrest in a dormitory here. You may not leave it without permission and you are sworn to silence on the matter of these proceedings. Remove the prisoner."

8

Ting, ting, ting, ting, ting, thud. The wooden incline had little bells mounted on it at regular intervals, and Galileo halted the pendulum as the ball struck the stop at the end.

"Papa, was it the same again?" Virginia cried out, ever keen to help her father in his observations. She loved the wood and metal smell of his workshop.

"Yes, child, it was," he said, bending down and picking her up.

"But why, Papa?"

"That I cannot say, my dear. It is indeed a mysterious force that moves objects of all sizes and weights at the same speed, indeed they even increase in speed at the same rate."

"You will find this strange mover, won't you, Papa?"

Galileo awoke at the sound of the large key turning the lock to his monk's cell. It was not yet light and so he could see nothing, then light spilt into the room from a candle as the door opened slowly.

"Bread and porridge from the refectory, Signor, and you have a letter," announced the servant he had been allowed to maintain, he placed the bowl on a small table and ignited the remains of a candle with the one he carried. When daylight eventually crept into the room, Galileo read the latest missive from Virginia. In the midst of her discourse on the household accounts and minor problems at *Il Gioiello*, she wrote about Vincenzio. She informed him that in order to accommodate his expanding family Vincenzio needed to buy a larger house but required his father's support to do so. Surely it was time for father and son to be reconciled? Galileo sat on the hard bunk and wept at the wisdom of his daughter, and the loss of his son and his grandchildren in the name of pride. In the knowledge that he might never see or communicate with his son again, he decided to be reconciled with him and provide the financial help Vincenzio and his family needed. After responding to Virginia's letter, he returned to re-reading the *Dialogue*. He could read for only one or two hours before his eyes began to tire from the effort of reading in poor light and his head ached with a terrible dull pain. He lay down and closed his eyes.

Guards crash into the room, push him against the wall and bind his hands behind his back. The rope bites fiercely into his wrists, his nose bleeds profusely. He is shoved and jostled along corridors, down stairs, across the cloister until he is outside again in Piazza Minerva, a crisp bright morning burns his eyes. He is surrounded by a squadron of soldiers and marched in this military bubble across Via Corso to Piazza Campo de' Fiori. All he can see are soldiers' uniforms, all he can hear is the sound of their marching. They stop, the leading soldiers move apart to reveal the piazza. A large crowd is at the end of the piazza and a group of Dominicans stand just in front of the soldiers, between the Fathers and the crowd a stake and pyre stands in terrifying isolation. His knees buckle, no one speaks, the crowd is silent. He is suddenly atop the pyre tied to the stake. A flaming faggot is placed in the pyre. He shouts, screams with all his strength: "Bruno! Bruno! Bruno!"

Galileo awakes with a start, out of breath, night has returned and stolen the light. Guards are not rushing in to the room. He has lost track of how long he has been a "guest" of the Holy Office, one, two, four days? Weeks? Eventually guards do enter the room and instructed Galileo to get up for a further discussion with the Commissary General.

"It's rather late for a deposition, isn't it?" said Galileo with bleary eyes.

"You may complain to the Most Reverend Father," sneered one of the guards.

This was the first time Galileo had seen his interrogation room in candlelight. Father Maculano was sitting at his desk, Father Sinceri was not present.

"Please sit." The Revered Father waved the guards away. Galileo was confused, not knowing whether this was irregular practice and would it be to his benefit or was it a trap. "Is this some additional deposition? Should we even be having a conversation without Father Sinceri being present? Do we need a notary?"

"Do you wish me to return you to your cell and leave you to the Tribunal?" Father Maculano snapped.

"No, I am sorry." The dancing light of the candles seemed to become somehow menacing.

"Your case is going badly for you." Galileo was stung by the obvious truth of this revelation. "I strongly urge you to change the tone of your depositions to one of recognition of error, perhaps suggesting ways in which your errors may be corrected. It is up to you of course, but be clear about one thing, the Holy Tribunal will find against you and so you should be prepared."

"How can you be so sure of this and why are you telling me?" asked Galileo, unsure whether or not to be angry.

"All of the minor charges against you, to do with printing and various other technical irregularities, have been withdrawn. The only remaining charge is whether or not you knowingly ignored the injunction of 1616: you have a letter from his Blessed Eminence Cardinal Bellarmino, the prosecution have an injunction signed by him and Commissary General Seghizzi. There is little doubt in my mind which view the Tribunal will take; if you want to survive this case you should start preparing the ground in a further deposition for your final abjuration." Galileo sat in stunned silence. "If you do not take this course of action you will be lucky if I can keep you in prison and away from the stake. Make it known to the court that you recognize your errors and are willing to abjure and I may be able to keep you alive."

Galileo gasped for air. "Why are you telling me all of this?"

"I do not wish to speak ill of my predecessor, but there is a lack of consistency in the records of Commissary General Seghizzi, in fact I am quite embarrassed by them. Furthermore, all of those minor, withdrawn, charges give this case a bad odour. I do not like the idea of authorities thinking that the Congregation of the Inquisition may be manipulated, no matter how exalted the puppet-master may be. That is all I have to say to you this evening. Guard! Please escort the prisoner back to his room."

The next day Galileo once again sat in the barrel-vaulted room before the Most Reverend Fathers Maculano and Sinceri, guards standing at his shoulders. He spent the night planning his speech and so had not slept, his great need for rest had been driven away by a desire to survive this case.

"Signor Galilei," Father Maculano said, "we have now received three depositions from you, do you wish to speak in your defence?"

"Yes, Most Reverend Father, I wish to make my possible errors known to you in the fullest light."

"Very well, proceed."

Galileo stood to recite his defence to full effect.

"During our first discussion of almost a month ago, I was asked if I had informed the Most Reverend Father Master of the Sacred Palace about the private injunction issued to me sixteen years ago by order of the Holy Office: 'not to hold, defend, or teach in any way whatsoever' the opinion of the earth's motion and the sun's stability; I answered 'No'. Since I was not asked the reason why I did not inform him, I did not have the opportunity to say anything else on the matter. Now I feel it is necessary to mention it further in order to prove the absolute purity of my mind.

"At that time, that is in 1616, some of my enemies were spreading the rumour that I had been summoned by Lord Cardinal Bellarmino in order to abandon some opinions and doctrines of mine, that I had to abjure, that I had received punishments and so on, so I begged His Eminence for a certificate explaining why I had been called to discourse with him; this is the document I earlier submitted." Galileo paused to allow Father Sinceri time to write as he spoke. "The certificate clearly states that I was told not to hold or defend Copernicus's doctrine of the Earth's motion and the Sun's stability; but other than this general pronouncement I was given no additional special order. Having in my possession this reminder, written by Lord Cardinal Bellarmino himself, I did not try later to recall or give any other thought to the words used to give me the said injunction orally. Thus when I hear the words of the injunction referring to 'teaching' and 'in any way whatsoever', these strike me as new and previously unheard. I do not think I should be mistrusted about the fact that in the course of fourteen or sixteen years I lost my memory of them, especially as I had no need to give the matter further thought having the certificate of His Eminence as a constant reminder. Now with these two phrases removed there is no doubt that the order contained in my certificate from his Eminence Lord Cardinal Bellarmino is the same as the injunction issued by the decree of the Holy Congregation of the Index. From this I feel very reasonably excused for not notifying the Master of the Sacred Palace of the injunction given to me in private." Galileo then outlined the tiresome process of gaining his imprimatur and that all due processes were followed, he also added that having re-read his own work he would concede that some arguments were too strenuously stated and that perhaps the *Dialogue* could be improved by the addition of two more days of discourse to fully refute the Copernican opinion.

"Finally, I am left with asking you to consider the pitiable state of ill health to which I am reduced, due to the constant mental distress of the past ten months or so, and the discomforts of a long and tiresome journey in the most awful season at the age of seventy. I am encouraged by the faith, clemency and kindness of heart of the Most Eminent Lordships, my judges." Galileo returned to his seat.

"We thank Signor Galilei for his comments. You may now return to your domicile with the Tuscan Ambassador until required to attend our presence again."

Galileo was escorted back to Palazzo Firenze, only to find that the Niccolinis were staying at the Villa Medici. The Palazzo staff had been instructed to look after Galileo's every need and send a message to Villa Medici when he arrived. He enjoyed a change of clothes, good wine and a little food; much as he desired a comfortable bed, he spent the evening preparing and rehearsing his abjuration, eventually dozing a little in a chair. Caterina arrived at the Palazzo early in the morning to see Galileo off and wish him well. He silently nodded and left with the escort.

Dressed in the white robes of the penitent, Galileo knelt facing his interrogators, Commissary General Reverend Father Maculano and prosecutor Father Sinceri. Along the wall to Galileo's right sat the ten members of the Holy Tribunal, the congregation sat in silence. The sun flooded the room with warm soft light, and decorated the floor with yellow squares and the sharp shadows of imperceptibly moving bars. Cardinal Borgia sat at the end of the row of

Cardinals, closest to Galileo. He stood and read aloud the outcome of the Tribunal.

"Whereas you, Galileo, son of the late Vincenzio Galilei, Florentine, seventy years of age, were denounced to this Holy Office in 1615 for holding as true the false doctrine taught by some that the sun is the centre of the world and motionless and the earth moves; for having disciples to whom you taught this same doctrine; for interpreting Holy Scripture according to your own meaning in response to objections based on Scripture which were sometimes made to you..."

Galileo's ears filled with the sound of blood rushing about his body, his gaze locked firmly onto Commissary General Father Maculano.

"We say, pronounce, sentence and declare that you, Galileo Galilei, because of the things deduced in this trial and confessed by you have rendered yourself according to this Holy Office vehemently suspected of heresy, namely of having held and believed a doctrine which is false and contrary to the divine and Holy Scripture: that the Sun is the centre of the universe and does not move from east to west, and that the Earth moves and is not the centre of the universe."

Galileo's pulse was racing, he could feel the damp advance of perspiration down his face, arms and back. His breathing became shallow, he was almost gasping for air but he managed to fight the urge to do so.

"We condemn you to formal imprisonment in this Holy Office at our pleasure. As a salutary penance we impose on you to recite the seven penitential Psalms once a week for the next three years. And we reserve the authority to moderate, change, or condone wholly or in part these penalties and penances."

He now waited for the signal from Father Maculano that he should make his abjuration. The moment arrived. "I Galileo, son of the late Vincenzio Galilei, Florentine, seventy years of age, arraigned personally for judgement, kneeling before you Most Eminent and Most Reverend Cardinals

Inquisitors-General against heretical depravity in all of Christendom..." He had rehearsed his curriculum vitae of misdeeds well and recited them with feeling. "I swear and promise to comply with and observe completely all the penances which have been or will be imposed upon me by this Holy Office; and should I fail to keep any of these promises and oaths, which God forbid, I submit myself to all the penalties and punishments imposed and promulgated by the sacred canons and other particular and general laws against similar delinquents. So help me God and these Holy Gospels of His which I touch with my hands." As he spoke, he pictured Virginia in the white robes of the novitiate taking her vows as a bride of Christ. "I, Galileo Galilei, have abjured, sworn, promised, and obliged myself; and in witness of the truth I have signed with my own hand the document of abjuration and have recited it word for word in Rome, at the convent of Minerva, this twenty-second day of June 1633."

Galileo was left kneeling in silence for some minutes before Father Sinceri rose to speak. "The penitent may return to his seat. This court is mindful of the prisoner's previous good character as a Catholic, his age and infirmity and has also received representation from eminent personages of the Tribunal. It has therefore decided that the penalty of life imprisonment will be commuted to a life sentence of house arrest. The prisoner's abjuration and sentence will be communicated to inquisitors, apostolic nuncios and pronounced in public throughout the country. You will be taken hence, under escort, to the home of Archbishop Piccolomini of Siena where you will spend the rest of your life. You may not leave this house, meet with visitors or entertain guests without the prior notification of the authorities, your domicile will be under the constant scrutiny of the local authorities. You may have not more than two days to conclude your affairs in Rome and proceed to Siena."

Relief washed over Galileo, he did not hear all that was said because he was already thanking the Lord for His infinite mercy.

9

Physically and emotionally drained, Galileo drifted through the small banquet the Niccolinis had arranged in his honour. The select gathering included cardinal Borgia and the pope's brother cardinal Antonio Barberini, both members of the Tribunal that just yesterday had condemned Galileo. However, Galileo knew these men had put themselves at some political risk by not voting with the Tribunal, indeed they had also canvassed for Galileo's imprisonment to be commuted to house arrest. Galileo could not remember the last time his heart and eyes felt so full of gratitude and humility.

Galileo hardly touched his food, barely supped his wine, he looked and felt like a man in a dream. Eventually, Francesco rose to present a toast.

"To our most honoured guest, may you yet provide the world with more of your wondrous insights and live a long and happy life. And, furthermore, you have the word of everyone around this table that as long as our bodies hold breath we shall be working to enable you to return home to your beloved Florence and *Il Gioiello.*" Everyone thumped the table and cheered loudly. Galileo's hand shook slightly as he silently raised his glass to his friends.

The journey to Siena was cold and miserable but otherwise uneventful. Archbishop Ascamio Piccolomini was a fine host with a great interest in Galileo's ideas; soon a small number of selected and trusted scholars and local nobles were regular guests, all taking part in fine intellectual discussion and debate with the Archbishop and his infamous guest. Galileo attended mass daily at the nearby San Matino; during his first few weeks in Siena he arrived early for mass in order to recite the penitential psalms daily rather than weekly. On the days when feeling particularly bitter and angry he forsook the Doxology and took some enjoyment from placing additional emphasis on the third psalm of the sequence:

> *But mine enemies are lively, and they are strong: and they that hate me wrongfully are multiplied.*
> *They also that render evil for good are mine adversaries; because I follow the thing that good is.*
> *Forsake me not, O Lord: O my God, be not far from me.*

During these journeys of penance out of the palazzo he was careful not to engage in any discussions; on his way to mass he scuttled like a thief past the Loggia del Papa so as not to be recognized or drawn into any discussion. He also avoided the Piazza del Campo, because he could never know who was watching or listening but he knew full well that the Vatican had eyes and ears everywhere. Indeed he found the streets of Siena simply too steep for his ancient frame to wander far away from the palazzo. Galileo did his best not to be noticed when roaming the tight, crowded, curving streets; he left the palazzo only to go to mass or to buy provisions to send to Virginia.

One evening, as the first ice cold rains of winter hammered Tuscany, Galileo and Ascamio were enjoying a glass of wine by the fire when the Archbishop suddenly asked, "Leo, I am curious about a certain rumour that has reached my ears, and I hope you do not consider my enquiry impertinent, but I am intrigued by the boldness of it if true." Galileo smiled and nodded his assent for the Archbishop to continue. "It has been said that after your abjuration, as you rose to stand, you said, soto voce of course, 'And yet it moves'. Is that indeed the case?"

Galileo grinned enigmatically. "When I taught at the University of Pisa, I would occasionally drop objects of differing weights down a stairwell, asking my students to positively identify which one hit the ground first. The object was to try to engage them in questioning the premise of Aristotle's theory that objects of differing weights will fall at differing speeds; it was of course a wasted effort in most cases as these students were usually only interested in how swiftly their wine or breeches fell. Anyway, it was often reported that I would carry out this exercise off the Torre Pendente of the Campo dei Miracoli, it being a convenient height and angle." Galileo returned to his wine, his grin an apparent echo of his recollections. The Archbishop tried to press his guest for a firm confirmation that the rumour was untrue, but without success.

"By the way, did I mention that I have begun to gather my thoughts and notes for a possible new book?" Galileo suddenly announced. Ascamio coughed and spluttered with surprise, thrilled and frightened in equal measures.

"Why, that is wonderful, Leo. Dare I ask the topic of this new work?"

"Don't worry, I am not writing about the heavens, my goodness I have been such a fool." The Archbishop was wise enough to know that silence was the best prompt for Galileo to continue speaking; he gently re-filled their glasses. "I spent so much time with my neck bent and straining towards the heavens in order to earn a place at court and prove why tides move that I neglected all of the work I started in Pisa. Those infuriatingly simple questions that seem almost impossible to answer, about motion or the strength of materials."

"Well, that sounds as though it might be safe from the prying interests of the Inquisition," Ascamio added hopefully.

"There are certainly no Scriptural worries in what I am considering but that's not the point, is it?" Ascamio did not respond. Galileo continued: "No, the point is Aristotle. I was brought before the Inquisition not on a dubious point of Scripture but because I was close to demonstrating that Aristotle was wrong about the heavens and that is what the Church could not accept. Surely the Jesuit defence of Aristotle must come close to being a veneration that should be reserved for Our Lord? Unfortunately, for the Collegio Romano at least, Aristotle was also wrong about motion."

Archbishop Ascamio ignored Galileo's rhetorical question, but could not ignore his jibe at the Society of Jesus. "Leo, I am deeply honoured that what I am sure will become a significant work was begun under my humble roof, but I beg you, I implore you to be careful about what you say. There is no doubt in my mind that you would not escape the clutches of the Congregation of the Inquisition a second time." Galileo nodded his recognition of the Archbishop's warning, and satisfied with this, Ascamio allowed his curiosity to press the conversation further. "But let us speak no more of such dark matters. Do you think you could explain, in simple terms, to an ignorant Churchman why Aristotle was wrong about motion?"

Galileo shuffled forward in his chair, eagerly grasping his full glass. "Aristotle says that the speed at which things fall will vary according to their weight. So if an iron ball and a wooden ball, half the weight of the iron one, are dropped from a height of one hundred cubits, the iron ball should land on the ground before the wooden ball has travelled more then fifty cubits. But in reality the wooden ball will land within a hand's width of the same time as the iron ball. No, I am sure that objects of differing weights dropped in a vacuum would land on the ground at exactly the same time. It is not weight but the resistance of the atmosphere that affects the speed at which objects fall. I can demonstrate, have demonstrated, but thus far only to my daughter, that objects of differing weights do fall at the same rate. Although, I have been forbidden from producing any more published books, I may collect some of my notes together, perhaps even arrange them somewhat. If someone else then considers that it may be worthwhile that these notes should be circulated in print I don't think I would be responsible for that particular book, do you? Anyway, I shall probably be deep in the ground by the time that happens and the Dominicans come looking for me again." Galileo spoke with a mischievous grin. "Let's recharge our glasses."

Heavy rain and thick cloud obscured Jupiter in the eastern sky.

ABOUT THE AUTHOR

Ian T Wyatt lives and works in Birmingham (UK). *Vatican File 1181: Galileo* is his first work of fiction and grew out of his interest in science. He has written on a wide range of subjects from rock climbing to shopping and education law to medieval Icelandic literature. His work is often detailed but wears its research lightly.

Made in the USA
Charleston, SC
19 July 2015